## 'You're  y fiancée, s '

'Of course ' ht smile and tried to pull herself together. What on earth was the matter with her? It would be fine. She was only playing a part, after all. Just a role of make-believe, nothing more. She could handle it.

'What's the matter?' Mark leaned against the kitchen table and gave her a boyish grin. 'Bowled over by the thought of me kissing you?'

Kissing her? She swallowed hard.

'You're planning to kiss me?' Her voice was little more than a croak and she cleared her throat and tried to look casual. 'Well, thanks for the warning. I'll try not to laugh.'

Then she changed the subject. Anything to avoid having to think about kissing Mark.

**Sarah Morgan** trained as a nurse and has since worked in a variety of health-related jobs. Married to a gorgeous businessman who still makes her knees knock, she spends most of her time trying to keep up with their two little boys but manages to sneak off occasionally to indulge her passion for writing romance. Sarah loves outdoor life and is an enthusiastic skier and walker. Whatever she is doing, her head is always full of new characters and she is addicted to happy endings.

**Recent titles by the same author:**

THE MIDWIFE'S CHILD
WORTH THE RISK

# THE DOCTOR'S ENGAGEMENT

BY
SARAH MORGAN

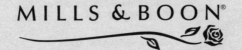

*First published in Great Britain 2001*
*Harlequin Mills & Boon Limited,*
*Eton House, 18-24 Paradise Road, Richmond, Surrey TW9 1SR*

© Sarah Morgan 2001

ISBN 0 263 82687 2

*Set in Times Roman 10½ on 11½ pt.*
*03-0901-51523*

*Printed and bound in Spain*
*by Litografía Rosés, S.A., Barcelona*

# PROLOGUE

'YOU want me to do *what*?'

Holly Foster sat down on the sofa with a thump and the phone slipped from her fingers.

'Holly—?' The deep male voice trickled out of the receiver. 'Holl, are you still there?'

She must have misunderstood him. Scrabbling around on the floor for the phone, she lifted it to her ear. 'I'm still here.'

'What's the matter?'

Holly blinked. 'I'm shocked, that's what's the matter! You asked me to…you want me to…' She took a deep breath and swept a strand of pale blonde hair out of her eyes. 'You were joking, yes?'

'No.' His voice was calm and steady. 'I've never been more serious in my life.'

Holly opened her mouth but no sound came out. Her voice seemed to have failed. She tried again. 'Let me get this straight. You're asking me to *marry* you?'

'Damn it, Holly, of course I'm not asking you to marry me!' He started to laugh. 'You're my best friend and have been for twenty-four years. I certainly don't want to marry you!'

'But you said—'

'I didn't say anything about marriage,' he drawled. 'Come on Holly! You know how I feel about marriage.'

She did know. It wasn't that Mark was against marriage, but she knew that he was quietly determined to find the right person first time round. They'd talked about it frequently over the many years of their friendship, sharing their dreams and hopes. It certainly wasn't a decision he'd ever take lightly. So why was he suggesting—?

'Mark.' Holly frowned suspiciously. 'Have you been drinking?'

'Drinking? It's seven o'clock in the morning, Holly,' he pointed out gently, and she yawned and glanced at the clock on the table. Seven o'clock? Only Mark would ring her that early. Not that it made any difference, of course. She'd been awake anyway…

'Well, apart from being under the influence of alcohol—' she forced her mind back to the conversation '—I can't think of a single reason why you'd be asking me to marry you.'

'You'll understand once I've explained, and I'm *not* asking you to marry me,' he said impatiently. 'You weren't listening properly. Wake up, will you? I didn't say married. I said engaged.'

'That's the same thing!' Holly stifled another yawn and tugged her skimpy nightie down over her slim thighs. 'Mark Logan, you are the last man on earth I'd choose to spend the rest of my life with! You're just not my type—'

'What do you mean, I'm not your type?' He sounded affronted. 'I'm supposed to be your best friend!!'

Holly grinned. 'You are my best friend—doesn't mean I'd want to marry you, though. Or pretend to be engaged, come to that.'

'Oh, come on, Holl,' he murmured persuasively. 'What's the problem?'

'What's the problem? Mark, people don't just *pretend* to be engaged,' Holly said emphatically. 'They either do it properly or not at all.'

There was a slight pause. 'We used to do it when we were children.'

'What, play mothers and fathers, you mean?' Holly

started to laugh. 'I was four and you were six if my memory serves me right. I think we've moved on a bit since then.'

But not much. Unlike Mark's, her love life was totally non-existent.

Resolutely she pushed the thought away. She had good friends and she was healthy. After everything that had happened in the last two months she was only too aware of what mattered in life. Romance, or rather the lack of it, was the least of her problems.

'I still don't see why you're shocked.' Mark wasn't taking no for an answer. 'It wouldn't be difficult.'

Holly shook her head and blonde hair wafted around her smooth cheeks. 'It would be impossible. It would never work.'

'Give me one good reason.'

She could give him more than one. 'Well, for a start you're in Cornwall and I'm in London. Hardly the basis for a convincing romance.'

'I've thought of that,' he said immediately. 'We need a practice nurse because ours is leaving. You can come here. Perfect solution for everyone.'

Holly gaped at the phone. 'You're asking me to move to Cornwall?'

'Absolutely.' He was arrogantly sure of himself, typically Mark. 'You'll love it, Holly. June in Cornwall is wonderful. Sea, sand, sailing…'

Tempting images filled her head and her eyes drifted to the window of her small rented flat which gave a bird's-eye view across the crowded, car-jammed streets of North London. She hadn't even thought about moving away. She frowned down at the stationary traffic locked bumper to bumper on the busy main road as people started the battle to get to work. But maybe that was the answer. Maybe if she moved, she'd leave the memories behind. Maybe, if she wasn't in London, she'd be able to sleep again.

'Just say, for the sake of argument, I uprooted myself and moved to Cornwall,' she said cautiously. 'It still wouldn't work. You and me pretending to be engaged, I mean.'

'Why wouldn't it work?'

She felt suddenly flustered. 'It just wouldn't. We've known each other for ever and we're not—not...'

'What are we not?' Mark started to laugh and, to her surprise, Holly found herself blushing. Mark had never made her blush before. Never.

'We're not...' she searched for the word, feeling ridiculously embarrassed '...loving. I mean, we hug and things but we certainly don't behave like lovers.'

There was a slight pause. 'We could if we tried. We may not be lovey-dovey normally, but there's nothing to stop us pretending.'

Holly frowned and nibbled her lip. Could she do that? She'd never thought of Mark as anything but a good friend. Pretending that he was her lover would be totally alien to the way she felt about him. Could she be convincing?

'I don't know, Mark. I'm not sure I could do it.'

There was a pause. 'Why not?'

He never took no for an answer!

Holly chewed her lower lip. 'Because I'm not in love with you, for a start!'

'Thanks, Holly!' Mark's voice was dry and tinged with humour. 'First you say I'm not your type, then you say you don't love me. You certainly know how to puncture a man's ego, I'll give you that.'

'Don't be silly. I love you as a friend, of course I do, but I don't...' Holly paused as she tried to explain. 'I don't love you *romantically*.'

'Well, who's going to know the difference? Friends is fine,' he said firmly. 'We'll just throw in a bit of touchy-feely for good measure.'

'Touchy-feely'? What on earth did he mean, 'touchy-feely'?

Holly twisted the phone cord round her slim fingers, still feeling uneasy about the whole thing. 'Even if I could be convincing,' she hedged, 'people have known us as friends for so long they'd never believe there was anything else between us.'

'Our friends in London might think that,' Mark agreed, 'but down here in Cornwall no one has a clue how we feel about each other so it would be easy.'

He'd obviously thought it all through.

Holly drew breath, her thoughts tangled. 'Why do you need a fiancée anyway? You said I'd understand once you explained. So—explain.'

There was a pause and Mark cleared his throat. 'There's this woman—'

Holly groaned. 'Oh, Mark, not again!!'

Whenever Mark Logan had a problem, it was always a woman. And sometimes more than one. The man attracted the opposite sex like no one else she'd ever met.

'Damn it, Holly, it isn't my fault!' Suddenly Mark sounded tired and frustrated. 'To be honest, I was trying to steer clear of women for a while. I only started this job five months ago—'

'Mark, I know that,' Holly said patiently. 'I'm the mug who helped you drag all your worldly goods down to deepest Cornwall, remember?'

And after that her whole life had fallen apart, but, of course, Mark didn't know that yet.

'I love this practice.' Suddenly Mark's voice was serious. 'I love the patients—the fact that most of them have lived here all their lives. I love the sea and the sailing. I even love the influx of tourists. Being a GP here is my dream job really.'

'So what's wrong?' Holly frowned. 'You've been fending women off since you were in primary school. I can't believe you've got a problem you can't handle.'

'I *can* handle it,' Mark said smoothly. 'I'm acquiring a fiancée. And fast.'

Holly's green eyes widened. It was beginning to fall into place. 'You want a fiancée to keep this woman at a distance? Isn't that overkill? Why not just tell her you're not interested?'

'I did, believe me. You know I'm always straight with women. But she doesn't want to hear it and, anyway, it isn't that simple.' Mark sighed and she could almost see him raking his fingers through his cropped dark hair. 'She works in the practice.'

'Ouch!' Holly pulled a face at the phone. 'You got involved with someone from the practice?'

There was a muffled curse. 'No, I did not! I am not "involved", as you put it. I did nothing! I haven't encouraged her, I haven't singled her out—I've been strictly professional.'

Holly thought for a moment. That was probably what had clinched it. 'Some women are very attracted to aloof men. Especially macho, aloof men who look like you. So how did it all start?'

'She invited me to the pub after work. I was expecting there to be a group of us. I thought she was just being friendly.'

'Mark…' Holly smothered a smile. 'Women are never "just friendly" with you. They lust after you, they fantasise about you and they behave in all sorts of strange ways to attract your attention, but they are *never*, absolutely never, "just friendly".'

'That's nonsense.' Mark's tone was clipped and she could sense him frowning. 'You're saying that a man and a woman can't have a platonic relationship.'

'No.' Holly frowned thoughtfully. 'I'm saying that a man like *you* can't have a platonic relationship.'

He muttered something rude under his breath. 'What's different about me?'

'Where do you want me to start?' Holly settled herself more comfortably on the sofa. 'You're the archetypal tall, dark and handsome male. To put it another way, you look like a film star, and as if that wasn't enough you're also clever, arrogant and cool in a way that drives women wild. One flash of that killer smile and they all succumb. Trust me on this one, Mark—you are just *not* the sort of man that women want a platonic relationship with.'

There was a stunned silence and then Mark cleared his throat. 'That's rubbish. Look at you and I for a start. We've been friends for ever.'

'That's different.' Holly gave a shrug. 'I've known you for twenty-four years and I don't see you the way other women see you. I'm immune.'

It was true. While other women had fallen heavily for Mark, she'd never seen him as anything other than her dearest friend.

'Oh, here we go again. More ego-bashing,' Mark drawled, his tone making it obvious that his ego was definitely intact. 'You're saying you don't find me attractive?'

'Why would you want me to? Mark, you're my best friend!' She rolled her eyes with exasperation. 'I'm not in the habit of fancying my best friend. Anyway, as I said before, you're not my type.'

'Why?' Suddenly he sounded curious. 'Go on—tell me. Why aren't I your type?'

'Oh, for goodness' sake, Mark, I don't know.' She frowned impatiently. 'I've never analysed it before. Basically because I don't go for macho males, I suppose. And you're very "male", if you know what I mean.'

'I'm not sure I do.' Mark started to laugh. 'Surely I'm meant to be "male"?'

Suddenly Holly felt flustered. 'What I mean is you're—you're—very rough and tough. You know, black belt in judo, accomplished sailor, rock climber. You like fast cars and—'

'You're basically saying I can't hold a conversation?'

'No.' Holly smiled and nestled deeper into the sofa. 'I'm not saying that at all. You're jolly good at conversation. I'm just trying to tell you why I don't fancy you. You're too macho. I prefer the sensitive sort.'

Actually, she didn't really know what she preferred any more. Her love life was such a disaster she'd given up analysing it.

'You don't think I'm sensitive?' Mark sounded hurt and she grinned, knowing it was a pretence. Mark wasn't that easily wounded. He was totally comfortable with himself, self-assured and confident in everything he did.

'You're sensitive with your friends. Just not your girl-friends. And it's not a post I've ever been interested in. And on top of that—' she played idly with the sleek curtain of blonde hair that fell over her shoulder '—I've known you since I was two and I remember the time when you put sand down my nappy—'

'Ouch. Surely I didn't do a thing like that.' His sudden laughter was infectious and she started to laugh, too.

'You did indeed. And when I was too old for nappies you put ice down my knickers, a snake round my neck and you cut off my pigtail to try out your new Swiss army knife.'

Mark was still laughing. 'What a lousy friend I must have been. OK, I get the message. In fact, I'm amazed our friendship has endured in the circumstances.'

'Well…' Holly's voice was gruff. 'I suppose I should

also add that you're a great listener, good company and the best friend a girl could want.'

Mark broke the long silence that followed. 'That's nice to hear. And it means you can definitely be my fiancée without me worrying that you'll expect me to marry you at the end of it.'

'Which brings us back to your story of the woman,' Holly prompted him, and he sighed.

'So it does. Anyway, we went out for this drink and she cornered me. I managed to escape without hurting her feelings but it's getting worse by the day.'

'Did you kiss her?'

There was an explosion of sound. 'No, I did not kiss her!!'

'Maybe you should have done. You should have given her a really horrid, wet, wimpy, slimy kiss that would have put her off you for ever.'

'I'm not sure I know how to kiss like that.' His voice shook with laughter. 'And if you know how that sort of kiss feels then you've definitely been going out with the wrong sort of men.'

Holly's smile wavered. She didn't need him to tell her that, but men and relationships were the last thing on her mind right now.

'OK.' She changed the subject quickly. 'So what's happening with this woman at the moment?'

He gave a groan. 'It's becoming embarrassing at work. I didn't want to be rude and ruin a working relationship, so I mentioned that I was engaged to you.'

Holly took a deep breath. 'Well, that's all right,' she said carefully. 'Other people have long-distance relationships. Just tell them I've got a job I can't leave.'

There was a long pause. 'It isn't that simple. They wormed the truth out of me, I'm afraid.'

'The truth?'

'That you left your job a few months ago and have done bits of agency work since. Unfortunately my confession coincided with our practice nurse leaving to have a baby, so they came up with the idea of you joining me. I was cornered really, but the more I thought about it, the more it seemed like a brilliant solution. If I have a fiancée down here in Cornwall, then this woman is more likely to leave me alone.'

Holly's mouth opened and closed. 'So they already think I'm coming? You didn't think to ask me first?'

If he hadn't been her dearest friend she would have put the phone down!

'I'm asking you now! In fact, I'm begging you, Holl!! Think about it,' he urged, his voice deep and persuasive. 'If I have a fiancée I don't have to spend every minute of the day wondering whether what I'm doing or saying could be misconstrued. I can just get on with my life.'

'But, Mark—'

'And you can get on with your life, too. You still haven't found a permanent job, have you?' He paused. 'You haven't told me why you resigned from your last practice nurse post, but I know something happened.'

Holly stiffened, and her heart rate bolted. Suddenly they'd moved onto dangerous ground. 'Nothing happened.'

'Come on, Holl, this is me. I know you better than anyone.' His voice was gruff. 'You're not the sort of person to leave a job without good reason.'

She'd had a good reason. A very good reason. 'I—It was nothing. Just politics.'

'Don't lie to me, Holly.' His voice was calm and matter-of-fact. 'I know something's wrong. And I know it's something big because it's the first problem in your life you haven't shared with me.'

He was right. It *was* the first thing she hadn't been able

to tell him. But he'd been miles away in Cornwall and it wasn't something she could talk about on the phone.

She bit her lip. 'Mark—'

'It's OK, babe,' he said softly. 'I know you'll tell me when you're ready. I'm just suggesting that whatever it was might heal faster down here. The job is yours for as long as you want it, and if you decide to leave when this is all over then fine. I know you're not happy just doing agency work—'

'It means I can pick and choose the jobs I do.'

Which was absolutely essential for her peace of mind.

'But that's not you. You like stability.' Mark was as astute as ever. 'So get yourself down here and then I'll be close by when you're ready to spill the beans.'

'I don't know, Mark,' Holly croaked, and there was a pause.

'Get yourself down here,' he ordered, his voice gruff and kind. 'That way I can keep an eye on you.'

Tears blurred her vision and she gave a watery smile, relieved that he couldn't see her. Just talking to him made her feel safe. If she was honest, she could do with a bit of Mark's protection right now.

'Maybe I should. You're a good friend.'

'Despite the snake and the ice?'

'Despite that,' Holly admitted, her voice choked.

'So come and be my fiancée and practice nurse.'

Holly thought for a long moment. 'What would it involve?'

'The job?'

'No.' For some unknown reason Holly felt her colour rise. 'The other bit. Just how ''touchy-feely'' would we have to be?'

'I don't know. Use your imagination.' He chuckled. 'Generally I would think it would be fine if you just hang on my every word, gaze at me adoringly and follow me round like a puppy.'

'Yuck!' His teasing made her feel better again. 'I don't think I could do that without being sick.'

And without feeling jolly uncomfortable. Pretending to fancy Mark would feel odd.

'You've done it before—'

'Mark, we've already established that we were in primary school at the time,' she reminded him dryly. 'Hardly the same thing at all.'

'Well, just do your best.' There was a brief silence. 'And you'd have to live with me, of course.'

'Live with you?' Her voice was little more than a squeak and Mark laughed again.

'Of course, live with me. This is the twenty-first century, Holly. People usually live together when they're engaged. Anyway, it's an ideal arrangement because you'd need somewhere to stay and it's impossible to get short-term lets in Cornwall in the holiday season.'

'I don't know, Mark.' Holly hesitated. 'What if it ruins our friendship?'

'Why on earth should it do that?' He sounded astounded at the suggestion. 'Holly, we've been friends for twenty-four years. Nothing has ever ruined our friendship.'

She frowned. 'But this is different, Mark.'

'"Always and for ever",' he reminded her softly. 'That's what we used to say to each other as children. Remember?'

Holly gave a soft smile. She'd never forgotten their childish promise to be friends for ever. 'Of course I remember, you idiot.'

'Then what's the problem?' His voice was gruff. 'Nothing has ever threatened our friendship, Holly. Not even when we've lived miles apart and had serious relationships with other people.'

Holly bit her lip. Serious relationships? She'd never *had*

a serious relationship. Not really. In fact, she was beginning to think that she must have totally unrealistic expectations about relationships because they were always such a colossal disappointment.

'We haven't lived together before.'

'So confess all your annoying habits, then.' He spoke in that lazy drawl that turned women weak at the knees. 'Do you leave the top off the toothpaste? Am I going to find your undies strewn over my radiators?'

'Surely that would be part of the fiancée role,' Holly quipped, and he laughed.

'Probably would. You see? You're more attuned to it than me.' There was a slight pause and when he spoke his voice was serious. 'I really need you, Holly. I'm sorry to do this to you, but say yes, babe. Please?'

Her protests collapsed in a heap. Mark needed her. And when had she ever been able to refuse him? He'd always been there for her. Always.

All he needed was a fake fiancée. He wasn't asking much really and, if she was honest, working with him again would be fun. She bit her lip. Maybe having Mark nearby would help her. Maybe living with him would get rid of some of the nightmares. Mark was so physically strong that it was hard to be nervous of anything with him around. Nobody threatened Mark.

'Holly?' His voice was sharp. 'Are you still there?'

'Yes, I'm here.' She took a deep breath. 'OK, Mark. I'll do it.'

'You'll do it?' She could hear the triumph in his voice and she smiled in response.

'I think I must be mad but, yes, I'll do it. I'll be your "fiancée".'

As Mark started bombarding her with instructions Holly tried to ignore the little voice inside her head which suggested that pretending to be in love with him might not be as straightforward as it seemed.

She agreed to meet the senior partner in London for an interview and then, providing all was well, travel down to Cornwall at the end of the week.

It would be all right, she told herself firmly. Of course it would. After all, they were only pretending. It wouldn't change their relationship.

Would it?

# CHAPTER ONE

HOLLY switched off the engine and stared at the modern red-brick medical centre with trepidation.

This was ridiculous. Utterly ridiculous. Why had she ever agreed to such a thing? It was never going to work. How could she walk into that surgery and greet Mark as if he were the love of her life?

She gave a groan. Why on earth hadn't they discussed things in more detail? She had no idea what Mark was expecting. He'd asked her to arrive at lunchtime on Friday, but he hadn't given her any more details. What was she meant to do? Throw her arms around him and kiss him passionately or was she meant to be reserved?

She must have been mad to agree to it!

But it was too late to change her mind now.

Reluctantly she climbed out of the car and walked across the car park, pinning a smile on her face as she pushed open the door that led to the reception area.

'Yes?' The blonde woman behind the desk gave her a cool look and Holly paused uncertainly. Hardly the most effusive welcome she'd ever received.

'I'm here to see Dr Logan.'

'Dr Logan has been called out on an emergency,' the receptionist told her briskly, 'and in any case you can't see him without an appointment.'

'I'm not asking for an appointment.' Holly took a deep breath as she tried to get past that icy façade. 'I'm—'

'He has a space next Thursday at four o'clock.'

*Next Thursday?* Holly frowned. And what happened if one of his patients was desperate to see him before that?

'As I said before, I don't need an appointment,' she told the woman, her voice still friendly. After all, they were obviously going to be colleagues and she didn't want to alienate her. 'I'm not a patient. I'm Holly Foster, the new practice nurse. I'm Dr Logan's—'

'Fiancée.' The blonde woman stared at her for a moment and Holly saw her mouth tighten. 'Of course. I should have guessed.'

Holly swallowed and managed a smile. 'Why should you have guessed?'

'You match his description perfectly,' the receptionist said, frowning slightly as her eyes drifted to Holly's left hand, 'although you're not wearing his ring.'

His ring? Oh, help! Neither of them had thought of that.

'I never wear a ring at work,' Holly said quickly. 'It's unhygienic and my last practice wouldn't allow it. I thought I might have to start work straight away so I put it on my chain.'

She patted her blouse, hinting that it was hidden under her clothing, a practice common among nurses. Fortunately for her, at that moment the doors of the health centre crashed open and the ring was forgotten as the reception area was filled with screams.

'Help me! Someone help my daughter. She needs a doctor.' A woman struggled towards them, clutching a small girl who was shrieking hysterically. 'She's been bitten by a dog.'

'We don't have a doctor on the premises,' the receptionist told her briskly. 'They're all out on calls. You'll have to drive to the Infirmary.'

Holly gaped at her and took charge.

'Let me have a look,' she said to the woman, smoothing the little girl's hair with a gentle hand. 'You poor thing! What a scary thing to happen. I'm Holly, what's your name?'

The little girl continued to sob hysterically and peered at Holly with scared eyes.

'It bit me,' she wailed, and Holly nodded.

'I know. And I'd like to try and make it better. What's your name, sweetheart?'

'Helen,' the little girl sobbed jerkily, and Holly's smile widened.

'Well, isn't that funny? You're a Helen and I'm a Holly. Both our names begin with H. Where did the dog bite you, Helen?'

The little girl took a shuddering breath. 'Arm.' She shrank away from Holly who nodded sympathetically.

'I won't touch it, sweetheart, not until you're ready. What we need to do is make it nice and clean and have a good look at it. There's a special room here for that sort of thing. And there are some lovely toys...'

She crossed her fingers that her predecessor had kept toys in the nurse's consulting room. Surely she did. Everyone did.

Holly turned to the receptionist, her smile friendly. 'If I could just use the treatment room, we don't have to make these poor people travel all the way to the Infirmary.' She turned to give Helen's mother an explanation. 'I'm the new practice nurse and technically I haven't started yet, but I can't see anyone minding if we sort Helen out.'

The set of the receptionist's mouth indicated that she minded a great deal. 'We're not an accident and emergency department.'

'No,' Holly agreed quietly, her voice firm, 'but if we're capable of giving the care required, without the patient having to make a long trip to hospital, we should give it. I'll assess the bite and clean it up, and hopefully by then one of the doctors will have arrived back from their calls and they can write up some antibiotics. Is there a white coat I could borrow, please? My uniform is still in my suitcase.'

Her shoulders stiff with disapproval, the surly woman marched out from behind the desk and walked down a carpeted corridor. Making a mental note to have a word with Mark about the attitude of his receptionist, Holly gestured to Helen's mother to follow her.

'This is the room you'll be using.' The receptionist flung open the door and turned to leave. 'I'll phone the senior partner to let him know that you're here.'

And try and make trouble, no doubt, Holly thought uneasily, watching the woman leave. Oh, bother. She didn't need that sort of aggravation in a new job.

'Take no notice of Caroline Duncan,' Helen's mother said, rolling her eyes. 'Her bark is worse than her bite.'

Holly wasn't convinced, but she gave the woman a smile. 'I do apologise for the fact I'm not in uniform, Mrs...?'

'Brown. But call me Alison, and I don't care what you're wearing as long as you can sort my Helen out.'

'Well, I'm just going to dig out a white coat and then I'll have a look at it,' Holly promised, glancing round as the door opened sharply and Caroline entered, carrying a white coat.

Holly thanked her warmly. 'Oh, and, Caroline, presumably I can access the notes on the computer?'

Caroline frowned as she turned to leave. 'Our computer system is very complicated. I expect you'll need to be trained before you can use it.'

Holly, who had been using computer systems all her working life, smiled easily, still doing her best to be friends with the woman. 'I'm sure I'll be able to muddle through. Thanks, Caroline.'

She slipped on the white coat and then spotted a basket of toys under the examination couch. 'Oh, look at these, Helen!' She dived under the couch and retrieved the basket. 'Have a little look at those for me and tell me what there is because I've never seen them before.'

The little girl delved into the basket and finally a small smile appeared as she pulled out a bright yellow helicopter with blades that spun round. 'There's a helicopter! I love helicopters.'

'I had one like that when I was small,' Holly chatted away, calming and distracting the little girl until she felt the time was right to look at the damage. 'Can I just take a look at that arm now, sweetheart?'

Helen nodded, still intent on playing with the helicopter.

'Is it awful?' Alison Brown bit her lip as Holly unwrapped the makeshift bandage she'd used to stop the bleeding. 'It bled such a lot.'

'I'll just take a look. How did it happen? Did the dog have an owner?'

Alison sighed. 'Yes, it belongs to Mrs Ellis, the librarian. It was Helen's fault really. I've warned her not to touch dogs she doesn't know, but she will go up to them and make a fuss—you know children.'

'I do indeed,' Holly agreed sympathetically. 'Don't tell me—this wasn't a cuddly type of dog.'

'Not at all,' Alison shuddered. 'It was tied up outside the supermarket and Helen was over there and patting it before I could stop her. To be honest, I didn't think about stopping to have words with Mrs Ellis after it happened. I just sprinted over here in a panic.'

Holly dropped the bloodstained bandage in the bin and examined Helen's arm carefully.

'Actually, it isn't very deep at all,' she said finally, walking across the room and rummaging through the cupboards until she found a dressing pack. 'The biggest risk from animal bites is infection, so what we need to do is clean it really carefully and then give Helen some antibiotics. How old is she?'

'She's five,' came the reply and Holly nodded as she ripped open the dressing pack.

'And is she fully immunised? Did she have all her child-hood jabs?'

'Oh, yes.' Alison nodded vigorously. 'I really believe in immunisations. She had everything going.'

'Good. Then she won't need a tetanus injection. Helen, I'm just going to clean your arm. It might sting a little bit. Fancy you liking helicopters. Do you know that in one of the hospitals I worked at, we had our own helicopter?' Holly chatted away as she cleaned the wound, knowing that thorough cleaning was as important in the prevention of infection as the antibiotics.

'A hospital had a helicopter?' As she'd planned, the little girl was so interested in her story that she virtually ignored the pain in her arm.

'That's right. I worked in London, and as it's such a big place with lots of traffic, they have a helicopter to go and collect people who need to see the doctor in a hurry.' Satisfied that the wound was as clean as it was going to get, Holly inspected the edges, deciding that it was better left to heal on its own without sutures. 'I'm not going to stitch this, Alison, because it would be distressing for Helen and, to be honest, after a bite like this it's better, if possible, to leave the wound open so that any infection can drain away.'

'I know this sounds like a stupid question...' Alison blushed and pulled a face '...but there's no risk of rabies, is there?'

'No.' Holly shook her head. 'Rabies isn't endemic in this country. We'd only consider taking preventative measures against rabies if she was bitten abroad or if the dog was imported. But seeing as you know the owner—'

'Yes, I do.' Alison's mouth tightened. 'And I'll be having words with her, believe me. Helen was wrong to have touched it, but Mrs Ellis shouldn't be leaving an animal like that in a place where children are tempted to touch him.'

Holly taped a sterile dressing in place and helped the little girl put her T-shirt back on.

'Did you go on the helicopter?' Helen's eyes were like saucers and Holly smiled at her.

'Not usually. I worked in the accident and emergency department, so we used to take care of the people after the helicopter had given them a lift. But I did go out on it a few times.'

'Wow!' The little girl hardly noticed as Holly carefully dressed the bite. 'Was it very high up?'

'Oh, very!' Holly's green eyes twinkled as she secured the dressing firmly. 'The people looked like dots and I could see into everyone's gardens. Now then, I'll just check your notes on the computer. What's your address, Alison, and who's your GP?'

'We're with Dr Logan.' Suddenly Alison's eyes brightened mischievously. 'And he's so gorgeous it takes your breath away! But perhaps you haven't met him yet, have you?'

Holly gave a wry smile. 'Actually, I have. I've been acquainted with Dr Logan's fatal charm since I was two years old. We were at school together and we trained at the same hospital so our paths are always crossing.'

And now they were engaged, albeit fictitiously.

'Well, all the women in Cornwall are totally besotted with him,' Alison told her with a laugh. 'He's lovely with the patients. Never makes you feel small and always acts as though he's got plenty of time.'

Holly smiled. 'He's certainly a good doctor.' She tapped away at the keyboard with sure fingers until she brought the right information up onto the screen. 'Oh, here we are. Tell me—' she kept her voice casual '—do you normally have to wait a long time to see him?'

She wanted to find out whether Caroline's comment was typical of the time it took to get an appointment with Mark.

'Well, that depends on the receptionist.' Alison gave a wry smile. 'Caroline works on the principle that if she makes you wait long enough you'll either be dead or better by the time your appointment comes round. The others are really nice and if it's an emergency they always seem to manage to squeeze you in.'

'That's good to hear,' Holly said lightly, checking in the records that Helen had no recorded allergies or any other relevant medical history. 'Is she allergic to any drugs, Alison?'

'No.' Alison shook her head. 'Nothing.'

'Right. I'm going to ask one of the doctors to write her a prescription.' Holly tapped away again. 'Can you wait for a few minutes while I find out when one of the partners is likely to be back?'

Just then the door opened and Mark strode in, a frown touching his dark brows. 'Holl?'

'Good afternoon, Dr Logan,' Holly said, her voice formal in case he hadn't realised she was with a patient. 'Helen had a bit of an accident with a dog but we've sorted it out.'

Mark grinned at the little girl and for a brief moment Holly saw him as other women must see him. Tall and athletic, with broad, muscular shoulders and laughing dark eyes. With his cropped dark hair and permanently shadowed jaw he was wickedly handsome, and Holly wondered what the staid old ladies of Cornwall thought of him. Then she gave a chuckle. They probably loved him. The ones on the ward always had. She watched him curiously. Alison was right, he *was* gorgeous. Gorgeous and sexy. It was just that she didn't usually see that when she looked at him. She just saw the Mark she'd known all her life.

'Hello, tiger.' His attention was focused on his young patient. 'Have you come to play with my toys again?'

'Holly rides on helicopters,' Helen said breathlessly, and Mark laughed.

'I know she does. Always has her head in the clouds does Holly. And what have you been doing to your arm?'

Helen's lip wobbled. 'Dog bit me.'

'You poor sausage.' Mark squatted down so that he was on her level, his dark eyes gentle as they locked with the little girl's. 'Did you bite it back?'

'Of course not, silly.' Helen giggled in spite of herself. 'It was furry.'

Mark pulled a face. 'Yuck! And how does that arm feel now?'

Helen stared thoughtfully at her new bandage. 'Better,' she said finally, and Mark smiled and ruffled her hair.

'Good.' He looked at Holly and raised an eyebrow. 'Stitches?'

She shook her head. 'I thought it was best to avoid them. I cleaned it thoroughly, though. She's covered for tetanus but she'll need some antibiotics as it was a puncture wound. I thought co-amoxiclav—she's not allergic to anything, I've checked.'

Mark blinked and then gave a crooked smile. 'I'd forgotten what it was like working with someone as efficient as you.'

Holly pressed the right keys on the computer and the prescription came out with a whizzing noise.

'The wonders of technology,' Mark murmured, signing it with a flourish. 'Here you are, Alison. We'll need to see that wound again—when do you think, Holly?'

Holly laughed. 'Well, seeing as I haven't even got my uniform on yet, I don't really know the setup here. Is there a dressing clinic or do I just do a general session?'

Mark frowned and thought for a moment. 'Routine dressing checks usually just get booked into your general sessions. Meg, our practice manager, will fill you in on when they are. Most mornings, I think, and then special clinics— asthma, immunisation and things in the afternoon.'

Alison scooped Helen up in her arms. 'Gosh, you're a lump! Too big for Mummy to carry around like this.' She gave the child a squeeze and lowered her gently to the floor, glancing at Mark while she did so. 'So what happened to Sister Hill? I thought the baby wasn't due for another two months?'

'It wasn't, but I'm afraid her blood pressure shot up and she was advised to rest so she decided to leave earlier than expected.'

Alison picked up her bag. 'Which left you in the lurch, I would have thought.'

'You can say that again.' Mark gave a wry smile and raked long fingers through his dark hair. 'But fortunately Holly has kindly agreed to step into the breach so we should be fine now.'

'Come back in three days and I'll check that wound,' Holly said. 'Sooner if it becomes inflamed or swollen, but it shouldn't because the antibiotics should prevent any infection.'

Alison nodded and thanked her again before ushering the little girl out and closing the door behind them.

'Thanks for dealing with them,' Mark said, and Holly grinned at him.

'To be honest, I was quite relieved. I was so afraid that our first meeting was going to be in front of the practice staff and we hadn't discussed what I was meant to do.'

'Do?' Mark leaned broad shoulders against the wall and started to laugh. 'What do you mean, "do"?'

'Well, you know...' Holly shifted uncomfortably. 'I wasn't sure if I was expected to—to...'

She started to blush, which felt ridiculous. Why should she blush in front of Mark when she'd known him for ever?

'To what?' Mark was still laughing, his dark eyes teasing. 'To rip my clothes off in Reception in front of the patients?'

'It's all right for you to laugh!' She put her hands on her slim hips and glared at him. 'Mark Logan, you'd better watch your step or I won't do this for you!'

He stifled the laughter. 'Sorry, Holl. It's just that I had this vision of you—'

'I don't want to know,' Holly said primly, switching off the computer and clearing up the mess left from the dressing. 'As it is, we have now been reunited in private, so we can avoid touching public reunions.'

'Shame.' Mark gave her a wicked grin, his eyes dancing. 'We could have run towards each other in slow motion like they do in the movies.'

Her eyes twinkled in return. 'With the sound of the sea in the background.'

'Something like that.' His smile was warm. 'It's really good to see you, Holly.'

'It's good to see you, too. Even if that handsome face of yours has got you into trouble again.'

'Don't!' He gave a sigh and held out his arms. 'Hug?'

She crossed the room and hugged him just as the door opened and Caroline Duncan entered.

Guiltily Holly tried to pull away, but to her surprise Mark held her tightly for a moment before releasing her with apparent reluctance.

'Sorry, Caroline.' His tone was easy and friendly. 'You must excuse us but we haven't seen each other for a while and we thought we were in private.'

It was a gentle reprimand for the fact that she hadn't knocked, but Caroline was far from apologetic. In fact, if anything she looked angry. Her colour was high and she seemed flustered.

'There's a man in Reception who came off a jet ski in the bay,' she said crisply. 'I was going to send him to the Infirmary, but—'

'Oh, I'll see him as I'm here,' Mark said, his tone pleasant but firm. 'I've finished my calls so it's only lunch he's disturbing and I don't usually get that anyway. Send him through to my room. Holly can give me a hand—we used to work in A and E together.'

Holly rolled her eyes. 'Perhaps I'd better get my suitcase out of the boot and unpack my uniform,' she said dryly. 'I seem to have started work immediately.'

Mark pulled a face and looked guilty. 'I wanted to give you the weekend to make yourself at home in Cornwall. Do you mind starting straight away?'

'Of course I don't.' Holly smiled and followed him down corridor to his consulting room, gasping as she saw the view. 'Oh, Mark! No wonder this is your dream job. How on earth can you concentrate on the patients with a view like that out of the window?'

The yachts and fishing boats bobbed in the bay and the coast path stretched enticingly into the distance.

'Nice, isn't it?' Mark dropped his bag by his desk and switched on his computer. 'Oh, well, I suppose we'd better see this patient now.'

Holly lifted an eyebrow. 'Do you do anything except minor accidents in this practice?'

'That's what happens in a holiday resort,' Mark told her ruefully. 'We get plenty of the ordinary routine stuff, too, but we'll tell you about that over dinner. We're meeting Ian Hughes, the senior partner, this evening.'

'Oh, yes, I met him in London. I really liked him.' Holly stared out across the bay. 'Where's your house?'

When she had helped Mark move five months earlier he had rented a small flat until he'd found somewhere more permanent. Now she was dying to see the house he'd chosen.

'You can't see it from here. I wanted you to come down before I bought it but you didn't answer the phone for about two weeks...' Mark looked at her quizzically and Holly

coloured and turned away, avoiding that penetrating gaze.
Mark saw too much.

'I—I had a lot on…'

'Right.'

She knew from his tone that he didn't believe her but,
good friend that he was, he didn't push her.

'So, is it far?'

'No, not really.' Mark walked across and stood next to
her. 'My surgery finishes at five-thirty and I'm off then
until tomorrow so if you can wait that long you can follow
me home.'

'Well, if I'm going to be here all afternoon I might as
well unpack my suitcase and see some patients,' Holly suggested.

Mark hesitated and then gave a shrug. 'If you're sure
you don't mind, that would be great.'

Holly frowned. 'Just one thing—I think Caroline's taken
an instant dislike to me.'

'Yes.' Mark's tone was guarded. 'She probably would.'

'She would?' Holly lifted her eyebrows. 'Why would
she? What have I done?'

'Done?' Mark dragged his long fingers through his dark
hair and sighed. 'You haven't *done* anything. The reason
Caroline doesn't like you is because you are my fiancée,
and she's the woman I was telling you about.'

# CHAPTER TWO

'OH, MARK, it's stunning!'

Holly stared at the house which was perched on the clifftop with views across the estuary and out to sea.

'Great, isn't it?' Mark helped drag her cases out of the boot. 'Wait until you see inside.'

Holly slammed the car door and followed Mark through the front door of the house and into a huge, glass-walled living room.

'Oh, my goodness.' She strolled over to the windows that hugged all three sides of the living room, giving an almost panoramic view. 'This is fabulous. How on earth did you manage to get your hands on this?'

'Right place, right time, as they say. Come and see my deck. The view's fantastic. If I crane my neck I can see my boat.' He gave her a smug grin and unlocked the French windows, opening up one side of the living room so that she could step onto the bleached wooden decking that curved around the house.

He was right. The view was breathtaking. She closed her eyes and breathed in the air, enjoying its salty freshness.

'Have you done lots of sailing?'

'Masses.' Mark dropped onto one of the solid wooden chairs that surrounded a large table. 'There's a GP in the neighbouring practice who's keen and he's been crewing for me.'

'Poor man!' Holly rolled her eyes and smiled. 'I remember sailing with you in our teens. It was a nightmare!'

Mark lifted an eyebrow. 'I thought you loved our sailing.'

'You yelled at me, Mark.' Holly paced along the deck and looked at the view in the other direction. 'This is fantastic.'

'Did I yell?' Mark sounded astonished and Holly turned and leaned against the balcony, wisps of blonde hair flying across her face as the wind gusted gently.

'Never mind that. Tell me about Caroline.'

'Later.' Mark stretched out long legs and his dark eyes narrowed as they fixed on her face. 'I want to know what's been happening to you. I haven't seen you for five months and phone calls aren't the same. Bring me up to date. How's your love life?'

'Oh, you know.' Holly gave a careless shrug. 'Still kissing frogs.'

Mark threw back his head and laughed. 'And not one of them has turned into a handsome prince?'

'Not that I noticed,' Holly quipped lightly, trying to skirt over the fact that her love life was totally non-existent.

'So you still haven't lost your virginity?' Mark gave her a gentle wink and she blushed prettily.

'Why on earth was I stupid enough to tell you that?' she muttered crossly, and Mark chuckled.

'Because we've always told each other everything.' He shook his head slowly, his face alight with amusement and incredulity as he looked at her. 'I can't believe some lucky man hasn't swept you off your feet.'

'Well, they haven't,' Holly said flatly, and Mark's smile faded.

'So is that what's wrong?'

Holly stiffened and turned to look across the bay. Anything rather than meet the sharp look in his eyes. Mark was far too perceptive.

'Nothing's wrong—'

'You're a lousy liar,' he said softly, suddenly serious.

'Holly, you've lost weight and you've got dark circles under your eyes. And don't turn your back on me.'

She hesitated and then turned to face him, her expression haunted. 'It isn't anything—'

'Holly!' his voice was a threatening growl and she gave a wry smile that cost her a great deal in terms of effort.

'Well, let's just say it isn't anything you can do anything about.' She coloured slightly under his intense scrutiny. She didn't feel ready to tell him yet.

'Is it work or a man?' His tone was blunt.

'Mark, it really doesn't matter—'

'Work or a man?' he persisted, and she sighed in exasperation.

'You don't ever give up, do you?'

'No.' His gaze was steady. 'So now you've remembered that, perhaps you'll answer my question. Work or a man? Surely it wasn't—what was his name? Simon. Are you still seeing Simon?'

'No.' Holly shook her head, securing strands of blonde hair behind her ear. 'No, I'm not.'

'Good thing, too,' Mark growled, dark eyes narrowed. 'He wasn't right for you. His eyes were too close together.'

'So were his affairs.' Holly's voice was quiet and Mark stared at her.

'He had affairs? While he was with you?' His jaw tightened and his expression was ominous. 'Give me his address—'

'Mark, no,' Holly interrupted him hastily, knowing that Mark was more than capable of tracking down Simon and defending her rather too vigorously. 'I don't need you to intervene—but thanks for the thought.'

Mark's anger was still evident. 'Were you in love with him?' His voice was sharp. 'Is that why you've got the shadows under your eyes? Did he hurt you?'

Holly shook her head and gave him a wan smile. 'No, I

wasn't in love with him. And, no, he didn't hurt me—not really, so you can dismount from your white charger.'

Mark watched her for a long moment, his eyes intent on hers. 'OK,' he said finally, a frown touching his brows, 'but if he isn't responsible for your drawn appearance, who is?'

'No one!' Holly wrapped her arms round her waist and paced over to the far side of the deck. 'It was nothing like that. Drop it, Mark. Please.'

She heard the chair scrape on the decking and the sound of his footsteps behind her, then strong hands curled over her shoulders.

'Which means it must have been work.'

'Please, Mark.' Her voice was barely a whisper and her eyes were closed. 'I really can't face thinking about it.'

He swore softly and she felt his hands tighten protectively on her shoulders.

'You know I'm always ready to slay your dragon,' he said gruffly. 'You only have to say the word.'

The memories came crashing down on her like the waves on the rocks below and she took a deep breath.

'Can we change the subject?'

'OK,' he said finally, his voice soft, 'on the condition that you put that weight back on and lose the shadows round your eyes. And on the condition that you remember that I'm here for you whenever you need a friend. We've never had any secrets from each other. Don't forget that, Holly.'

How could she forget? He was her oldest and dearest friend. She turned to face him and for a wild moment she was tempted to confide in him. But she wasn't ready to talk about it yet. Not even to Mark. The truth was, she didn't want to think about it at all…

She lifted her chin and tried to lighten the mood. 'You're worried about the shadows under my eyes? You're saying I'm not glamorous enough to be your fiancée?'

He lifted a hand to stroke her hair away from her face, staring down at her with an odd expression on his face.

She tipped her head to one side. 'Mark?'

He stirred himself. 'You look great. I'm just worried about you that's all.' He turned away from her and walked back towards the French windows. 'OK, back to practicalities. We're going to the yacht club for supper with Ian, but we're not meeting him until eight-thirty so how about having a snack?'

She nodded and followed him inside, through the spacious lounge and into the kitchen.

'Mark Logan, you're a slob!' She surveyed the dirty dishes strewn around the work surfaces with mock disapproval. 'You have a perfectly good sink with a view to die for and you can't be bothered to wash up.'

'I told you I needed a fiancée,' he teased, his smile dying as he saw the look on her face. 'Just joking—truly!'

'Don't do your chauvinist act with me,' she scolded, tugging open doors in the kitchen. 'I can't believe this state-of-the-art kitchen doesn't have a dishwasher.'

'Last cupboard on the right,' Mark said meekly, watching as she pulled it open and started clearing the worktops and loading the dishwasher. 'Can I get you a drink? Wine? Gin and tonic?'

'Actually, just a cup of tea would be great, thanks.' Holly straightened and glanced round the surfaces which were now clear of dirty crockery. 'No wonder you need a fake fiancée. No one in their right mind would take on the role in real life.'

'I'm sorry. What with work and the boat, I've been busy.' He looked sheepish as he made the tea and handed her a mug. 'Sandwich? Biscuit?'

'Nothing, thanks.' Holly sipped her tea and wandered back into the living room. 'This place is amazing. It's like being part of the ocean.'

'Glad you approve. When you've finished your tea, I'll show you the upstairs.'

Once she drained her mug, they made their way up an unusual spiral staircase and Mark pushed open a door. 'This is the spare room. Your room, I suppose.'

It was a bright, cheerful room, decorated in blue and white, with a very nautical theme. Holly fingered a piece of driftwood thoughtfully. 'This is nice. Where did you find it?'

'On the beach. I go for a run most mornings before the rest of the world is awake. It's surprising what you find.' He turned and walked back onto the landing. 'Come and see my room.'

Holly gasped as she entered the master bedroom. Again the architect had made the maximum use of windows and the room was drenched in the soft early evening sunlight.

'Oh, Mark!' She paced across the bleached wooden floor covered in a soft rug and gazed around the room. 'It seems a waste to use this room for sleeping.'

'My sentiments exactly.' Mark gave her a grin that was pure predatory male and she rolled her eyes.

'You're terrible, Mark Logan!' She laughed and then frowned at him with mock disapproval. 'Are you still leading innocent females astray?'

'Absolutely not,' Mark said firmly, his eyes still gleaming wickedly. 'I can honestly say that I've never had anything to do with an innocent female in my life, and I've certainly never led one astray.'

'So bring me up to date on your love life.' Holly looked at him expectantly and he gave a short laugh.

'To be honest, there hasn't really been anyone since I moved down here. I've given up on women. I've decided that my perfect woman doesn't exist.'

Holly touched his arm gently and gave him a soft smile.

'She exists, Mark. Just hang in there. Maybe you're looking in the wrong places.'

'Probably. Still, it's history now.' He gave a careless shrug. 'As I said, I'm totally off women.'

'You? Off women? I'll believe that when I see it.' Holly gave him a wry smile and moved towards the window, giving a gasp of delight as she looked outside. 'You've got a balcony! Can I go out?'

'Of course. Key's in the drawer.' Mark retrieved it and unlocked the door for her, watching as she stepped out onto the balcony and breathed in the sea air with a sigh of appreciation.

'I love it. Truly, I love it.' She stared across the estuary for a long time and then stirred herself. 'Right, then. I suppose I'd better move myself into my room.'

Mark frowned and hesitated. 'I was thinking about that…'

'What?' She closed the door firmly and locked it, returning the key to the chest of drawers.

'How would you feel about keeping most of your stuff in my room?' he asked finally, giving her a wary smile. 'It's just that if anyone visits, they could easily stumble into your room and if they see that all your stuff is there…'

'Then we've blown our cover,' Holly finished for him. It sounded logical. So why was she blushing? To hide her discomfort she changed the subject. 'That's fine. Perhaps you'd better tell me about Caroline now.'

Mark sighed and closed his eyes. 'I suppose I'd better. Let's grab some drinks and nibbles and go and sit on the deck.'

'Good idea.' Holly followed him down the stairs to the kitchen and they piled snacks and a bottle of wine onto a tray and took it out onto the deck.

'OK, tell me the gory details.' Holly settled herself comfortably on one of the chairs and waited expectantly as he yanked the cork out of the bottle of wine and took a deep breath.

'Well, Caroline has worked at the surgery for about a year, from what I can gather. Only part time, but everyone treats her with kid gloves because she's had such a rough time. It's common knowledge so I'm not breaking a confidence by telling you that—'

'That's fine, Mark.' Holly's voice was soft. She knew that he would never gossip or do anything unethical. If he was telling her this then there must be a reason.

'It's pretty sad really.' He poured wine into a glass and passed it to her. 'Apparently she was engaged to some man—was crazy about him by all reports—and he stood her up at the altar. Literally. Just never turned up on the day, no explanation, nothing.'

'Oh, no!' Holly gave a gasp of horror. The poor woman. That was an awful thing to happen to anyone.

'It affected her really badly.' Mark sat down and stretched long legs out in front of him. 'It was a huge wedding with most of the town present, so it was a pretty awful thing to do.'

'Wicked,' Holly agreed, her green eyes appalled. 'So what happened to poor Caroline afterwards?'

Mark shrugged. 'Well, she'd resigned her job because he'd promised to take her travelling, but Ian took her back.'

'That was nice of him.'

Mark nodded slowly. 'He's a nice guy. It must have been a difficult decision for him really. He's incredibly supportive and loyal towards his staff, so he would have wanted to take her back, but deep down he must have known that she was going to take a long time to recover from something like that. It was bound to have a negative effect on the practice.'

'You said "was".' Holly raised her eyebrows. 'Isn't it a problem any more?'

'Well, she seems to be getting better.' Mark stared thoughtfully across the estuary. 'Lately we've all seen an improvement in her mood. Despite the way she behaved to you this morning.'

Holly shrugged. 'She wasn't so bad.'

Mark gave a wry smile. 'But, then, you never see bad in anyone.'

'That's not true—it's just such an awful thing to happen to anyone.' Holly murmured, her expression troubled. 'I'm not surprised she wasn't welcoming. Especially if the reason she'd cheered up was because she'd suddenly found another man she was attracted to.'

'You're very perceptive.'

'Not really.' Holly gave a shrug. 'I suppose she felt as though she could never find another man attractive, and then suddenly you come along, handsome and generally gorgeous, and her heart lifts slightly, only to be dashed into the ground when she discovers you're not interested.'

'Don't!' Mark raked long fingers through his dark hair and gave a long sigh. 'I feel guilty enough already without you spelling it out.'

Holly reached across and squeezed his hand. 'I'm sorry—I didn't mean to make you feel guilty. It isn't your fault. You can hardly have a relationship with her out of pity. I'm just saying it's a sad situation.'

'I know that,' Mark said gruffly, his eyes closed, his thick dark lashes touching his angular cheeks. 'And the truth is, it didn't happen exactly the way you suggested. Apparently she'd started to recover, and she'd been on a few dates with Greg—that's the GP I was telling you about that I sail with—and then she saw me.'

Holly gave a sigh. 'What is it with you and women?'

'Not my fault!' He gave her a black look. 'Anyway, she stopped seeing Greg and seemed to develop this wild, almost teenage crush on me. Horrendous! Maybe I should have just been blunt with her, but I didn't want to hurt her feelings so I thought it would be gentler if I just said I was already involved.'

'And a fictitious fiancée seemed the most gentle approach…'

Mark opened her eyes. 'Did I do the wrong thing?' Suddenly he looked unsure. 'You're a woman, Holly, you know how the female mind works. Was I wrong?'

It was the first time in her life she had ever seen Mark question a decision he'd made.

'No,' Holly said finally. 'I don't think you did the wrong thing. I think it's an impossible situation really. Whatever you did, her feelings would have been hurt. But we can't pretend to be engaged for ever. Sooner or later you'll get fed up with not being able to seduce women and we'll have to part company.'

'I'm off women at the moment,' Mark muttered, helping himself to some cashew nuts. 'And by the time you and I "part company", as you put it, I hope things will have moved on and she'll have realised what a nice chap Greg is. I've been working on it, subtly.'

'You? Subtle?' Holly put a hand over her mouth to suppress the giggles. 'Sorry. You are many things, Mark Logan, but subtle certainly isn't one of them.'

Mark stopped chewing and pretended to look affronted. 'Are you insulting me?'

'Probably.' Holly nodded, her eyes still alight with humour. 'Do you really think you should be matchmaking?'

'I'm not really matchmaking.' Mark shrugged and pulled a face. 'If it weren't for me, I'm sure they'd be together anyway. I'm trying to remind her that she was interested in him—that there are plenty more fish in the sea.'

'Plenty more fish in the sea? I'd love to know where they're hiding.' Holly picked up her drink and took a sip.

'I only find the equivalent of whelks and clams. I'm still waiting to meet a glossy trout.'

Mark laughed and his dark eyes teased her. 'In that case, no wonder you're still a virgin.'

She poked her tongue out at him. 'I never, ever should have told you that.' Hastily she changed the subject. 'So, go on. Tell me more about Greg.'

'Well, he's the chap I sail with.' Mark leaned across the table and took an olive. 'He's a partner in a practice on the other side of town. I even thought maybe we could make up the occasional foursome to try and bring them together again if it doesn't seem to be working out.'

Holly thought of the look that Caroline had given her when she'd arrived. 'I'm not sure she'd relish my company.'

Mark gave a crooked smile. 'She will once she knows you better.'

'I hope you're right.' Holly gave him an affectionate look. 'I must say, I'm very proud of you for being so sensitive about her feelings.'

He lifted an eyebrow. 'I thought you said I was incapable of sensitivity?'

'You are normally,' Holly said honestly. 'Well, at least when it comes to people who fancy you.'

'Am I really that bad?' He gave a short laugh. 'The truth is, I felt sorry for her—and a bit responsible. I didn't want to make things worse.'

Holly blinked. 'Mark Logan, there's hope for you after all.'

'Must be old age,' Mark said with a sigh. He slouched lower in his chair and rested one ankle on top of a powerful thigh. 'I'm obviously losing my sense of perspective. Here I am, having dragged you all the way down here to pretend to be crazy about me—hell, is it going to work?'

'Of course it is,' Holly said firmly, determined to make

it work now she understood the situation more clearly. 'We can easily pretend to be engaged. As you said, we know each other well enough, don't we?'

His smile was wry. 'Absolutely. Come on, let's unpack the rest of your stuff and get changed for supper.'

'But what about tonight? We haven't worked out what we're going to say.' Holly put a hand on his arm, feeling the solid muscle under her fingers. She'd forgotten how strong Mark was. Suddenly, for the first time in months, she felt safe. 'If I'm supposed to be engaged to you, we need to decide on a story. Ian didn't ask me anything personal when I met him on Tuesday, and frankly it's just as well. I haven't got a clue what I would have said!'

Mark frowned. 'No story. We'll just stick to the truth and that way we can't go wrong. The only bit we change is that, instead of staying friends, we fell in love.'

Holly swallowed. She still hadn't got used to the idea. 'When, er, did we realise that we were in love?'

They wandered back inside and Mark locked the French windows. 'About a month ago? That fits with what I told Caroline. When I moved down here to work, we realised how much we missed each other and how in love we were. How does that sound?'

'And we got engaged immediately?' Holly bit her lip and Mark shrugged his broad shoulders.

'Of course. Why not? We'd already known each other for ever so there was hardly any need to hang around. All of a sudden we discovered we were madly in love—cue the violins—I proposed, you accepted and that was that.'

'Where?'

'Where what?' Mark grabbed her suitcases from the hall and lugged them up the staircase, the muscles in his arms bunching under the weight.

'Where did you propose?'

'Holly, no one is going to ask a question like that,' he

protested, slinging both suitcases into his bedroom. 'Let's store your stuff in my room and just use yours for sleeping.'

'Fine. But, Mark, they will ask.' Holly flicked open a bulging suitcase and started unpacking. 'People are interested in that sort of thing. Especially women.'

He sighed. 'Well, where would you want to be proposed to?'

Holly tipped her head to one side and thought carefully. She couldn't imagine loving anyone enough to get to the proposal stage. But this was just make-believe, she reminded herself. So what was her dream? She closed her eyes.

'On a beach,' she breathed. 'Just the two of us. Twilight.'

'Sandy or pebbles?'

Her eyes flew open. 'What?'

'The beach,' he prompted, his dark eyes twinkling. 'Sandy or pebbles?'

'Mark, for goodness' sake!'

'You wanted detail,' he pointed out, 'so sandy or pebbles? Can we make it sandy? I don't want bruised knees if I'm proposing in traditional style.'

'Wimp.' She laughed, her green eyes dancing. 'All right. Sandy.'

'But where was this beach? We can't say it was Cornwall or they'll all be offended that they weren't introduced to you before.' He frowned thoughtfully. 'So perhaps I took you somewhere incredibly romantic to propose. Somewhere close enough for us to have slipped away for a weekend without people getting suspicious. How do you fancy Corsica?'

'Very much.' Holly laughed. 'Oh, my goodness!' She clapped her hand over her mouth and Mark lifted an eyebrow.

'Now what?'

'A ring!' She stared at him. 'Caroline asked me about it

and I made some feeble excuse. We hadn't thought of a ring.'

'I had.' Mark strode across the bedroom and rummaged in a drawer, retrieving a small black box. 'Here we are. I hope it fits.'

Holly opened the box and gasped at the stunning diamond that glinted at her. 'Mark, I can't wear this! It's real!'

'Of course it's real.' He gave her a taste of that grin that always had women drooling over him. 'You don't think I'd give my fiancée a fake, do you?'

She licked her lips. 'But…'

His smile faded and he brushed her cheek with his finger.

'It was my grandmother's,' he said quietly. 'She gave it to me to give to the woman who finally made me give up bachelor status.'

Holly stared at the ring. 'Mark, what if you meet someone you—you like and you're pretending to be engaged to me—what will you do?'

'Let's just say that, after my experiences with Zoe, I'm avoiding relationships for a while.'

Holly gave him a sympathetic smile. 'I'm sorry that didn't work out,' she said gruffly, and Mark gave a careless shrug.

'I'm not. She was gorgeous to look at but distinctly lacking in other qualities. She definitely had a short shelf life.'

Holly frowned disapprovingly. 'Mark! That's an awful thing to say.'

'No, it isn't,' he disagreed calmly. 'She was no more in love with me than I was in love with her. I never once misled her about my intentions.'

Which, knowing Mark, would have been purely physical. Holly felt her cheeks warm.

'Glad to hear you're still a virgin, too,' she murmured dryly, and he gave her a broad grin that was totally male.

'You know me, babe—pure as the driven snow.'

'Oh, yes!' She rolled her eyes to indicate what she thought of that statement. 'Try not to break too many hearts, Mark.'

'Me?' He pretended to look hurt. 'I'm always very kind to women.'

He was certainly kind to her but, then, she'd never been in love with him. She glanced at the ring and took it out of the box carefully, slipping it onto the third finger of her left hand.

'It fits.'

'You're right. It fits perfectly.' A strange look crossed Mark's face as he lifted her hand and examined the ring. 'What about you, Holl? What if you meet Mr Right while you're wearing my ring?'

'Mr Right is always in a different place when I'm around.' Holly twisted the diamond on her finger and Mark gave a low curse and hugged her. 'You'll tell me about it one day and I'll sort him out.'

'Don't be silly!' She pushed him away. 'Talking of which, are you still doing judo?'

'Not since I left London,' he admitted, 'but I could still get the better of the louse. Just give me his name.'

'There is no name.' Holly smiled. 'Stop playing boy hero and let's finish our cover story. We got engaged, and then what? When are we getting married?'

Mark frowned. 'Can't we leave that open? It'll make it easier when we have to break up anyway. Just say that it depends on our jobs and that sort of thing.'

'I suppose that sounds all right.' Holly shrugged. 'In that case I'll go and get ready. How dressy is the yacht club?'

Mark reached into his wardrobe and pulled out a pair of fawn trousers and a pristine white shirt. 'Quite dressy.'

Which meant digging through her rather limited wardrobe to find something that would suit Mark's 'fiancée'. Normally the man dated models and women who spent half their days in beauty salons. Holly glanced down at her short, practical nails in despair. She just wasn't Mark's type. How was she ever going to be convincing?

The yacht club was situated just beyond the fishing village with views across the headland and the estuary.

Mark pulled into the car park and Holly grinned as he parked his beloved sports car carefully by a low wall.

'Have you ever found a woman you love as much as this car?' she teased, and he pulled a face.

'Definitely not.' He looked across at her and his eyes narrowed. 'By the way, you look great. That colour suits you.'

She was wearing a strappy, green silk dress that looked good with her blonde hair and showed more than a hint of bare leg. As they walked into the yacht club, female heads turned to look at Mark and Holly was doubly glad that she'd made an effort with her appearance.

The restaurant was already filling up and Mark smiled and lifted a hand to a man sitting at one of the best tables.

'There's Ian.' He led her across the restaurant and shook hands with the older man. 'How are you, Ian? You've already met my Holly.'

My Holly.

For a minute Holly felt a strange feeling in her stomach and then she dismissed it and smiled warmly at the senior partner.

'It's nice to see you again.' She felt slightly shy, but the older man immediately put her at her ease.

'I can't say how delighted we are to welcome you here, my dear,' he said, pulling out a chair for her and seating her before he returned to his own chair. 'We were desperate for a practice nurse and when Mark told us his own predicament—how he'd just got engaged but you were so far away—it all seemed too perfect to be true.'

'I'm glad to help,' Holly said quietly, suddenly feeling a flash of guilt that they were deceiving this nice man. 'You must fill me in on what your main priorities are in the practice and tell me exactly how you want me to spend my time. We didn't really talk about the detail when we met in London.'

'Oh, plenty of time for that,' Ian said cheerfully, waving to a waiter and ordering them some drinks. 'Have a menu, Holly.'

The evening passed quickly and Holly found herself chatting openly to Ian, telling him about her childhood in London and how she and Mark had known each other virtually all their lives.

'Our parents lived next door to each other and were great friends,' she told him. 'Mark and I went to the same school and then trained in the same hospital, although Mark was there before me, of course. I suppose I've known him all my life really.'

'And you suddenly discovered that you were more than friends.' Ian sat back in his chair and put down his knife and fork. 'That's lovely. They always say that the very best relationships start with friendship. My wife would love your story. I'm afraid she couldn't join us tonight because she's babysitting our grandchild, but you'll meet her soon.'

Holly blushed and felt horribly uncomfortable. Could she keep this up?

'Why don't we fill Holly in on the different clinics?' Mark suggested smoothly, clearly aware of her discomfort.

Holly glanced at him gratefully. 'That would be very helpful.'

'The clinics?' Ian watched the waiter clear their plates. 'Well, the main one is our coronary heart disease clinic. We have a surprisingly high rate of coronary heart disease in this area. I say surprisingly, because one wouldn't expect it of a fishing port, but there you go!'

'So you run a clinic?' Holly shook her head when the waiter offered her the dessert menu. 'What sort of clinic? Screening?'

'Actually, more of a lifestyle clinic, although there is some screening involved.' Ian ordered coffees and smiled at Holly. 'As you well know, a myocardial infarction—or heart attack as the layman calls it—is part of a chronic disease process. There is some evidence that behaviour modification counselling increases healthy lifestyles.'

Holly nodded. 'I know that patients who have already had a heart attack seem to benefit from secondary prevention clinics.'

'Absolutely.' Ian murmured his thanks as the waiter poured the coffee. 'Which was how our lifestyle clinic started. We run it as a team—dieticians, GPs, health visitors, practice nurse—and we give each patient their own personalised lifestyle plan. It works brilliantly.'

'In fact, it works so brilliantly,' Mark interjected, 'that nearly all the other neighbouring practices have started to do the same thing.'

Holly sipped her coffee. 'So if someone needs dietary advice they see the dietician and if they're smoking—'

'Then we give them counselling directed at behavioural and attitudinal change,' Ian finished. 'And, of course, we use nicotine replacement if it's appropriate. Have you had any training in behavioural counselling?'

'Oh, yes.' Holly played idly with a teaspoon. 'The course I did trained us to assess whether a patient was ready to change and to use things like goal-setting and specific behavioural advice.'

'I knew you were going to be an asset.' Ian smiled and continued, 'As well as diet and smoking, we also look at their levels of physical activity. In fact, we even joined forces with the leisure centre and were offering different grades of exercise classes at one point, but unfortunately the instructor had a nasty car accident a few months ago so that's fizzled out.'

Holly tipped her head on one side as she listened. 'I could do that,' she said impulsively, glancing shyly at Mark. 'I'm a trained aerobics and keep-fit instructor, remember?'

'So you are.' He looked at her thoughtfully. 'I'd totally forgotten that. She's right, Ian, she could take some of the classes.'

Ian was delighted. 'Lots of the women in particular have been quite upset at missing their exercise sessions, so that would be fantastic.'

Holly blushed. 'Well, that's fine, then. When does it all happen?'

'We do the lifestyle clinics one evening a week and we all help out so it's pretty busy, but it seems to work.'

'Presumably there's a group discussion element, too?' Holly asked. 'Allowing people to talk about any problems they've been having or any worries?'

'We haven't done that to date...' Ian frowned thoughtfully. 'But it would be a great idea. I'd never thought of it, to be honest. We've always just seen people as individuals, but I think it would be very popular. The patients already meet up and chat informally while they're waiting to be seen. It would need someone to chair it, of course. I don't suppose I could tempt you?'

'You probably could.' Holly smiled, pleased to help. 'Perhaps with one of the dieticians because I'm sure some of the problems will be around weight control.'

'That would be excellent.' Ian beamed at Mark. 'I can see why you love this woman. Not only stunningly beautiful but clever and enthusiastic as well.'

Stunningly beautiful? Not by any stretch of the imagination, Holly thought, catching Mark's eye and trying not to laugh.

'Tell me about the other clinics,' she prompted, draining her coffee cup. 'Immunisation obviously. What's the uptake like around here?'

'Well, like most practices, we were affected by the MMR scare. We put quite a bit of work into educating the mums and our uptake has gone up again. How did you handle it in your last practice?'

'Much the same way,' Holly told him. 'We held a few open evenings, with the immunisation officer and the public health director answering questions.'

'And Mark tells me you used to work in A and E together.'

'That's right.' Holly smiled and exchanged a warm look with Mark. They'd had a lot of fun working in A and E.

Ian nodded. 'And then you joined an inner city practice in London. That must have had its stresses.'

Holly's heart started to race and her smile froze. She'd been careful at the interview not to discuss her reasons for leaving her last job in too much detail, and so she could only murmur an agreement whilst hiding her shaking hands in her napkin.

'Holly's a brilliant practice nurse,' Mark interjected smoothly, his sharp gaze fixed on her pale face. 'She's already seen several patients for us today.'

'Yes, Caroline rang and told me.' Ian frowned briefly and then smiled. 'It was very kind of you to step into the breach, Holly.'

'My pleasure.'

'Well, I know you're going to fit in well,' Ian said cheerfully. 'And I can see just how happy and natural the two of you are together. You're obviously a perfect match. So welcome to Cornwall and Harbour Medical Centre.'

Holly relaxed and smiled in response, and her eyes met Mark's. He was looking at her with a warmth and affection that made her heart turn over, even though she knew he was just acting.

What would it be like to have a man look like that at you and mean it? Especially a man like Mark?

Flustered, she glanced back at Ian, thinking again what a nice man he was. Slightly overweight, in his late fifties, Holly guessed, he was cheerful and solid and she was sure he'd be an excellent senior partner. She could see now why Mark was so attached to this place. It was wonderful. And she could see why he was so desperate to sort out the problem of Caroline. But was this ever going to work? Could she be convincing?

# CHAPTER THREE

To Holly's relief, Caroline had the first part of the week off, which gave her a chance to settle in and get to know the other members of the team without worrying about her relationship with the other woman. She was relieved to find that things were run along similar lines to her old practice, which meant that, professionally at least, she felt confident.

On a personal basis she felt anything but confident. In front of his colleagues Mark treated her with total professionalism combined with a hint of warmth which suggested a more intimate relationship, and at home he was the same Mark she'd always known. In fact, she couldn't fault him—so why did being around him make her so nervous?

Despite her qualms the week flew by, and after lunch on Thursday Holly prepared for her first immunisation clinic.

'We generally have a very good turnout on both a Thursday and a Friday.' Debra Flint, the health visitor, was busy checking the list. 'Oh, good, little baby Watts is due for his first lot of jabs today. I'm worried about Mum, to be honest, so I'll be pleased if she turns up. She seems very depressed.'

'Is it her first baby?' Holly checked through the fridge for the various vaccines.

'Yes, and she's been very low, but she had an awful delivery so that's hardly surprising.' Debra frowned. 'I must talk to Mark about it because he was the one that referred her back to the hospital.'

Holly began to sort out some 'certificates of bravery' which were always helpful for the older children. 'What happened?'

'Well, she had a forceps delivery which went wrong and her bowel was perforated. Very nasty.' Debra fiddled with her pen thoughtfully. 'I have to say that the hospital was pretty hopeless. Mark was the one who diagnosed the problem in the end. You wouldn't believe what he said to the hospital! Let's just say he didn't mince his words and they sorted the problem out pretty sharpish.'

Holly gave a short laugh. 'I can imagine.'

'Well, of course you can, how silly of me.' Debra gave her an apologetic smile. 'You're engaged to him, for goodness' sake. You know better than anyone that he doesn't tolerate sloppiness. He's one of the brightest, most thorough doctors I've ever worked with. You're a lucky girl.'

Holly blushed slightly. 'Oh—Yes, I know.'

Oh, help! She hoped Debra didn't want a sisterly chat about her relationship with Mark.

'Anyway, Anna Watts has been pretty down ever since the birth.'

Holly frowned. 'Isn't there a questionnaire you use to diagnose postnatal depression—the Edinburgh scale or something?'

'The Edinburgh postnatal depression scale, that's right.' Debra tucked her pen back in the pocket of her blouse. 'She refused to do it last time I saw her and she hasn't been to clinic since. I can't seem to get near her to develop a relationship, although fortunately Mark saw a lot of her when she delivered eight weeks ago. She does seem to trust him, which is good. But all the same I'm relieved to see her name on the list today. It'll give me a chance to have a chat with her.'

Tina, one of the receptionists, popped her head round the door. 'The waiting room is like a nursery and the children are driving us mad. Are you ready to start?'

Debra grinned. 'Let battle commence!'

For the next two hours Holly was kept busy, reassuring

anxious mothers, soothing screaming babies and giving various immunisations according to the age of the child.

One mother in particular, Sylvia Bates, was very anxious about her thirteen-month-old daughter having the measles, mumps and rubella injection.

'I've read such awful things about MMR,' she confessed. 'If I have her done and she's damaged in some way I'll never forgive myself. I don't know what to do.'

Holly gave a sympathetic nod. 'It seems like a difficult decision, I know, but the number of children who have had a bad reaction to immunisation is such a tiny minority of the millions who have been immunised.'

Sylvia bit her lip. 'But can you guarantee there's no risk?'

'No,' Holly said honestly. 'All vaccinations carry an element of risk, but you have to measure that against the risk of the illness itself. Measles, mumps and rubella are highly infectious diseases, and if children catch them they can suffer serious problems.'

'But you so rarely see those diseases now,' Sylvia murmured, and Holly gave a gentle smile.

'And that's thanks to the success of our vaccination programme.'

'That's what my mum says,' Sylvia mumbled. 'A cousin of hers died of measles when my mum was young but, of course, we don't see it any more so you forget it can be serious.'

Holly nodded. 'Absolutely.'

Sylvia gave a groan. 'Oh, I don't know what to do…'

'What does your husband think?'

'He leaves all the decisions like that to me.' Sylvia rolled her eyes. 'Men! Oh, well, I suppose I'd better have her done.'

Holly frowned slightly. 'Don't feel coerced, Sylvia. It's important that you feel comfortable with your decision.

Would you like to go away and think about it and come back on another occasion?'

'No.' Sylvia shook her head. 'Definitely not. If she caught the illnesses I'd never forgive myself. Just do it, please!'

Debra scribbled down the batch number of the immunisation in the child health record and Holly quickly gave the injection.

'There we are.' She handed the child a toy and gave Sylvia a patient information leaflet. 'She may be a little fractious tonight and with MMR they sometimes develop a mild reaction seven to ten days after the injection.'

Sylvia tucked the leaflet into her handbag. 'What sort of reaction?'

'They sometimes get a rash and a fever,' Holly explained. 'The leaflet gives you all the information you need, but if you have any worries at all, just give us a call.'

'Thanks.' Sylvia scooped up the toddler and her handbag and made for the door. 'And thanks for taking the time to explain.'

'You're welcome,' Holly said quietly, and Debra looked at her with admiration as the door closed.

'Gosh, you're good at that.'

'Good at what?' Holly popped the needle into the sharps bin and washed her hands.

'Good at giving a balanced explanation,' Debra said. 'You listened to her fears and you gave her the facts without forcing her in either direction. I gather you've had a lot of practice at it.'

'Well, the last MMR scare that was in the papers certainly affected people badly, and who can blame them?' Holly frowned and shook her head, her blonde ponytail swinging jauntily. 'Those scare headlines do nothing for the confidence of the public.'

'I know.' Debra crossed Sylvia's name off her list. 'We

had a similar problem with that HRT scare. The surgery phone never stopped ringing and the doctors spent an entire week seeing nothing but worried women taking HRT.'

'So how are we doing?' Holly glanced over her shoulder. 'Just Mrs Watts left?'

'That's right.' Debra stood up and adjusted her blouse. 'I'll give her a shout.'

Anna Watts was a pale, quiet girl in her mid-twenties and she arrived with the baby in a car seat.

'How have you been, Anna?' Debra asked gently, helping her unstrap the baby from the car seat.

'Fine.' Anna lifted the baby up gingerly and settled him on her lap, holding the small bundle awkwardly.

Holly frowned. New mothers weren't usually so uncommunicative. Of course, Anna might just be a shy person, but still...

'I'm the new practice nurse,' she said gently, her green eyes warm and friendly, 'and we haven't met before. The baby's beautiful. Boy or girl?'

'Boy.' Anna stared down at the bundle in her arms, her expression blank.

'And what's he called?' Holly dropped to her knees so that she was closer to baby and mother.

'Harry.'

'Nice name.' Ouch. Anna Watts clearly didn't want to talk at all, and all Holly's instincts were telling her that Debra was right and the woman was depressed. She seemed totally uninterested in anything, including the baby. 'I don't have any children, but I've always thought it must be very hard, adjusting to being a mum all of a sudden.'

Anna looked at her properly for the first time. 'It is.' Suddenly her eyes filled with tears. 'And I'm no good at it. I'm a hopeless mum.'

'Oh, Anna!' Impulsively Holly put an arm round the thin shoulders and gave the other woman a comforting squeeze.

'That's not true at all! Just because it seems hard, it doesn't mean you're no good. Look at Harry—he's healthy and happy. That's all down to you.'

'She's right,' Debra said gruffly. 'You *are* doing a good job, Anna. But you're obviously feeling very down, aren't you, love?'

Anna started to sob. 'I just can't cope,' she choked. 'I don't get any sleep, I have a permanent headache, I've got no one to help me, and sometimes when Harry cries and cries I think I might do something to him. It's not that I don't love him—but sometimes it just gets too much.'

'I can imagine.' Holly made soothing noises and comforted her while Debra lifted the baby away from the distraught mother.

'You poor thing. Does Harry cry a lot?'

'In the evenings it's a nightmare,' Anna confessed, her voice choked. 'He yells non-stop for three hours. I know he's got tummyache but I can't seem to help him. I've tried colic drops but they didn't work at all.'

Holly frowned thoughtfully. 'How about massage?'

'You mean rubbing his tummy?' Anna looked doubtful and Holly nodded.

'It can be quite effective for colicky babies, can't it, Debra?'

Debra nodded. 'There are some mothers who find that it works wonders. There's a local group for baby massage which started a few months ago. If you like, I could try and find their number.'

'No, thanks.' Anna shook her head and blew her nose hard. 'I—I don't really feel like meeting anyone right now.'

Holly bit her lip. The poor, poor woman! She glanced at Debra and then back at Anna.

'I could pop round some time and help you,' she said quietly. 'I could bring some oils and we could do it together. If you wanted me to, that is.'

Anna hesitated. 'Would you do that?'

'Of course,' Holly said immediately. 'I'd be glad to. I can't promise it will help, but it's worth a try. Is that all right with you, Debra?'

'Absolutely!' Debra was obviously relieved to have found someone else to help with Anna, and Holly was pleased that the other woman obviously wasn't territorial about her patients.

'I think if I could stop him crying such a lot I'd be able to cope better,' Anna confessed, the tears falling again.

'Does your husband know you feel like this?' Holly handed her a handful of tissues.

'He knows I'm a bit down.' Anna shredded the tissues and made a visible effort to stop crying. 'But he's just lost his job and it's all very stressful at the moment. He goes out with his friends a lot and I sometimes wonder if he's staying away on purpose because things are so awful at home. I just haven't got anyone to turn to.'

Holly exchanged looks with Debra. 'Would you consider joining a postnatal group Anna? It might help you make some friends. Meet people in the same situation.'

'I really couldn't.' Anna's shoulders shook with sobs once again. 'I haven't got the energy to go out. I really haven't.'

Which was most likely the reason she wasn't turning up at clinic and Debra wasn't seeing her.

'What about family?' Holly probed gently. 'Are any of your family nearby?'

Anna shook her head again. 'There's only my dad and he's in his seventies. And Bill's mum and dad are too far away to help.'

No wonder the woman was exhausted. Holly ran through the options in her head. One thing was certain—Anna couldn't be allowed to leave until they'd found a way to help her.

'We need to sort this out one stage at a time Anna,' Holly said gently. 'I'll come round and see if massage helps Harry's colic, but we need to think about *you*, too. Who's your GP?'

'Dr Logan,' came the reply, and Holly nodded.

'And have you tried talking to him about how you feel?'

'Oh, I couldn't!' Anna wiped her swollen eyes and sniffed. 'He was great after Harry was born and I had all those problems, but this is different. He's a man and he hasn't got children of his own. He'd be really shocked if he knew some of the things I've been thinking about Harry. He couldn't possibly understand.'

'That's not true,' Holly said swiftly. 'Not only is Dr Logan a superb doctor but he's also the uncle of twins, and they're the biggest handful you've ever met. Believe me, he wouldn't be shocked by anything you told him. He knows what hard work children can be.'

'I just couldn't. What would he think of me?' Anna started to sob again and Debra frowned.

'He wouldn't think anything, pet. He wouldn't judge you if that's what you're worried about.'

Anna's breath was jerky. 'He might think I'm an unfit mother.'

'Anna, you're a lovely mother,' Holly said gently. 'You're just very down and you need help. And Dr Logan can give it. Please, let him.'

Anna sniffed again, clearly hesitant. Just then there was a tap on the door and Mark popped his head round.

'I wondered whether you'd seen—' He broke off and his sharp eyes narrowed as he registered what was happening. 'Anna?'

He closed the door behind him and crossed the room in two easy strides, squatting down next to Anna, his handsome face concerned.

'What's the matter?' His voice was kind and Anna swallowed hard.

'It's nothing—really.'

'Come on, Anna,' Mark said softly. 'You don't cry over nothing. You must be feeling pretty low.'

Anna hesitated, tears threatening again as she struggled for control and shredded another tissue between trembling fingers. 'I—I know it's stupid...'

'It isn't stupid at all.' Mark's voice was steady and calm. 'If I'd been through what you went through I'd be feeling low, too.'

'It's my fault,' Anna whispered. 'I should try and snap out of it.'

Mark shook his head, his dark eyes holding hers. 'It's not your fault at all. If it's anyone's fault then it's probably mine for not checking up on you sooner. I should have guessed you might feel depressed after the awful time you had. How long have you been feeling this bad?'

'I—I don't know really.' Anna's voice cracked and the tears spilled down her pale cheeks. 'It just seems to have got worse and worse.'

'I'm really sorry,' Mark said gruffly, taking her hand in his and giving it a squeeze. 'I should have followed you up more closely. Why on earth didn't you come and see me?'

Anna bit her lip. 'I didn't want to be a bother.'

'Oh, Anna.' Mark gave a groan and rubbed his forehead with long fingers. There was a pause while he mentally ran through the options. 'OK, here's what we're going to do. You're going to come with me now, and we're going to have a cup of tea and a chat. Then you're going to promise me to come and see me every week until I see you laughing.'

Anna's eyes widened. 'You can't spare the time to have a cup of tea with me. You've got patients to see.'

'You're my patient, too, Anna.' Mark straightened and gave her a gentle smile that did funny things to Holly's insides. How many doctors did she know who would have handled the situation so sensitively? Not once had he dismissed Anna's feelings, made her feel stupid or let on that he was in the middle of a busy surgery. Mark was so good with people and such a good doctor.

'We just need to give Harry his first immunisations,' she told Mark quickly, and he nodded.

'Fine. Bring her through when you're ready.'

Holly turned back to Anna with a smile. 'Are you happy about Harry having his immunisations? Has Debra explained it all?'

Anna nodded. 'Yes, she gave me a booklet. Does he have the meningitis injection as well?'

'Yes, although the vaccination only covers meningitis C,' Holly told her, drawing up the injections quickly. 'I'm afraid there still isn't any protection against meningitis B so we all have to stay vigilant.'

'You'll think this is a silly question,' Anna mumbled, 'but he can't catch meningitis from the injection, can he?'

Holly shook her head, her ponytail swinging. 'No. And it isn't a silly question at all. But the meningitis C vaccine isn't what we call a "live" vaccine. In other words, there's nothing in it that can cause the disease.'

'Oh.' Anna gave a weak smile. 'Well, I'm happy for him to have it in that case.'

Holly gave the injections quickly and took advantage of Harry's outraged yell to squeeze the polio drops onto his tongue. Then she helped Anna carry her belongings through to Mark's consulting room.

'Do you want me to tell your patients that there'll be a wait?' She spoke quietly to Mark and he shook his head.

'I've finished surgery,' he told her. 'I've got some house calls but there's nothing that can't wait for half an hour.

I've asked Tina to call them and let them know I'll be delayed.'

By the time Holly arrived home that evening she felt exhausted and took advantage of Mark's absence to strip off her uniform and climb straight into a hot bath.

By the time she heard his key in the door, she'd changed into jeans and a bright blue strappy top and was putting the finishing touches to an exotic salad.

'Mmm. That looks delicious.' He peered over her shoulder and reached down to steal an olive. 'I can see why I'm marrying you.'

She thumped him playfully. 'In your dreams, buster! You look hot and bothered. Go and change. Wine or beer?'

'Oh, beer, please.' He groaned and dropped his length onto one of the kitchen chairs. 'I haven't got the energy to get changed yet. What a day!'

'So how was Anna in the end?' Holly's voice was soft and he gave a rueful smile.

'In a pretty bad way. Bad enough for me to give her an antidepressant. I've spoken to Debra and she's going to see her twice a week for counselling until she improves slightly. And I gather you're going to try massage on the baby. That was nice of you.'

'No problem. I thought I'd give her a call tomorrow to arrange it.' Holly handed him a beer and then mixed oil and vinegar for the dressing, thinking how tired he looked. 'I don't know much about postnatal depression. How do you tell the difference between a normal reaction to suddenly having a new baby and proper depression?'

'The answer is, with difficulty,' Mark admitted, taking a mouthful of beer, 'but in Anna's case I'm totally confident that she's suffering from a clinical depression. She has low mood, lack of interest, loss of enjoyment—she's permanently tearful and she can't concentrate. Fairly classic signs.'

Holly added a touch of mustard to her dressing. 'And is it safe to take drugs if you're breastfeeding?'

Mark pulled a face. 'Well, all antidepressants are secreted in breast milk to some degree, but in this case it's irrelevant because she never managed to breastfeed. And that gives her yet another thing to feel depressed and guilty about.'

'Poor thing.' Holly bit her lip and picked up the pepper mill. 'Didn't they help her in the hospital?'

'The hospital,' Mark said grimly, tapping the can on the table, 'were hopeless in Anna's case. In every way possible.'

'No wonder she's depressed.' Holly added yoghurt to the mixture and poured it into a jar. 'She was so upset today. And she seemed very lonely. You were lovely with her, Mark—she really trusts you.'

He gave a short laugh. 'That's probably because I was the only doctor who took notice of her original symptoms, poor thing. I'd only been with the practice for a couple of months, but I spent a lot of time with her after she was discharged because she was in such a mess. I suppose I got to know her quite well.'

'It's just as well you did,' Holly said softly, 'because she doesn't trust anyone else yet.'

'No. She's very isolated at the moment.' Mark leaned over again and stole a piece of salami. 'Debra's given her a list of groups she could join.'

Holly bit her lip and looked at him, feeling troubled. 'But when you're depressed it's hard to make yourself do anything that proactive.'

'That's true, but Debra will keep an eye on her,' Mark said confidently, unbuttoning his shirt and revealing a hint of tanned male chest covered in curling dark hairs. 'And I'll be seeing her every week, too.'

For some reason the brief glimpse made Holly feel oddly uncomfortable and she looked away quickly. What was the matter with her?

She put the oil and vinegar back in the cupboard and took a deep breath. It was this silly pretence, that was all. It was making her think about Mark in ways she'd never thought of him before. So it was best not to think of him at all. She forced her mind back to the subject of Anna.

'Aren't you anxious about her?' she asked, regaining control.

'Holly, I've done what I can.' His voice was gentle but firm. 'I can't spend every spare minute worrying about every patient I see or I'd go nuts. I have to switch off, I'm afraid. It's a survival mechanism. It doesn't mean I don't care. It just means I'm doing my job properly. Getting too involved is bad news—you should know that.'

Holly nodded and twisted the lid onto the jar, shaking the dressing vigorously. 'Go and change and I'll finish dinner.'

'Thanks. It's the lifestyle clinic tomorrow so we'll both be busy with that, but I'll cook on Saturday.' Mark helped himself to another olive and frowned suddenly as he stood up. 'Oh, not Saturday. I knew there was something I'd forgotten to tell you. It's the beach barbecue.'

Holly put the dressing down on the table and stared at him. 'What beach barbecue?'

'They have it every year and it's on Saturday.' Mark shrugged apologetically. 'Sorry. It slipped my mind. It's a sort of social night with everyone from the practice and the other neighbouring practices.'

Holly blinked. It sounded daunting. 'Do—do I have to come?'

What were they all expecting of her? So far she and

Mark had only been seen together in a professional capacity.

'Don't you want to?' His eyebrows lifted. 'You're supposed to be my fiancée, sweetheart, remember?'

'Of course I am.' She gave him a bright smile and tried to pull herself together. What on earth was the matter with her? It would be fine. She was only playing a part after all. Just a role of make-believe, nothing more. She could handle it.

'What's the matter?' Mark leaned against the kitchen table and gave her a boyish grin. 'Bowled over by the thought of me kissing you?'

Kissing her? She swallowed hard.

'You're planning to kiss me?' Her voice was little more than a croak and she cleared her throat and tried to look casual. 'Well, thanks for the warning. I'll try not to laugh.'

Studiously avoiding his gaze, she spooned capers into the salad and walked over to the sink to wash some baby tomatoes.

It wouldn't be a proper kiss, she reassured herself. Not in public. Just a little peck. She'd been pecking Mark all her life, so there was nothing to worry about.

'Can't imagine kissing you really.' Mark narrowed his eyes as he studied her. 'It will feel a bit like kissing my sister. Gross, as my oldest nephew would say.'

'Oh, thanks, Mark!' Holly threw a tomato which landed with a satisfying plop in the middle of his solid chest. 'You're so good for my ego. And talking of sisters, how is Julie? Are the twins still a handful?'

She changed the subject neatly. Anything to avoid having to think about kissing Mark.

'They're several handfuls,' Mark said dryly, stooping to pick up the tomato before strolling towards the door. 'How Julie copes I will never know. I only survive my visits because I know the end will come eventually.'

Holly laughed, knowing that he didn't mean it. She'd seen him in action with his sister's children and he was wonderful with them.

'Oh, well…' He glanced down at his shirt and pulled a face. 'I suppose I'd better do some first aid on my shirt. Remind me not to tease you again. You're a lethal shot with a tomato.'

Holly waved a spoon at him threateningly. 'You should see me with a blunt instrument!'

'Hey, less of that.' He pretended to glower at her. 'You should be practising for Saturday. You're meant to play the part of my adoring fiancée, not a nagging wife.'

'Adoring?' Holly pinned a worried look on her face. 'You want adoring? Ouch. That could be a challenge. How long have I got to practise?'

'Holly…' He started to laugh. 'You're starting to worry me. You're supposed to be madly in love with me. Right now, you're being less than convincing.'

'Yes, well.' Holly was a picture of innocence. 'To use your own words, the thought of being an adoring fiancée is pretty gross.'

'Gross, eh?' He grinned and started to saunter towards her. 'In that case, perhaps we'd better have a practice before Saturday.'

Her smile faded and she backed away rapidly. Suddenly he seemed very big and very male. She most certainly didn't want to practise.

'No need.' Her voice was little more than a squeak. 'I'll practise in front of the mirror later.'

'Well, call me so that I can watch.' He flicked her cheek with a careless finger and glanced at his watch. 'Have I got time for a shower before supper?'

'Of course.' Holly managed a casual smile, limp with relief that he hadn't tried to kiss her. Oh, for goodness' sake! What was the matter with her? This was Mark! Just

Mark! Why was he making her feel so nervous? It was the whole situation, she decided. She'd been friends with Mark for more than two decades and trying to pretend to be anything different felt strange.

That was all it was. Nothing else. It was just uncomfortable, examining their relationship.

She finished preparing the salad and tried to ignore the uneasy feeling in her bones. Saturday would be the first time they'd really had to act as a couple. But it would be easy, she told herself firmly. It was just Mark after all…

# CHAPTER FOUR

THE following evening Holly attended her first lifestyle clinic, along with Ian, Mark and a pretty dietician called Samantha.

'All the patients coming to this clinic have had a previous myocardial infarction,' Ian told her as they prepared for the clinic together. 'The idea, really, is to give them ongoing support and encouragement. So if they're trying to lose weight or stop smoking, we try and help in whatever way we can. That might be by using behaviourally oriented counselling, or just by giving moral support. I liked your idea of running a group discussion. Would you be prepared to start that tonight if people are keen?'

'Of course.' Holly gave him a swift smile and quickly checked that she was familiar with all the literature they were giving out. 'This looks much the same as the material we used in my last practice, so there shouldn't be a problem there.'

'I use some of my own diet sheets,' Samantha told her, delving into a large bag and bringing out a handful of booklets. 'They're usually popular because they're pretty straightforward and easy to understand.'

Holly took the leaflets from her and glanced through them. 'Oh, yes, these are good.' She tucked a wayward strand of pale blonde hair behind her ear. 'If we run a discussion group we could always get the patients to suggest recipes. If we collect enough we could do a practice recipe book.'

'That's a fantastic idea!' Ian grinned at Mark. 'Your fiancée is jolly creative, isn't she?'

'She's amazing,' Mark said softly, an intent look in his dark eyes as they fixed on her face. 'And what about the exercise class, Holl? Did you ring the leisure centre?'

'Yes.' Holly blushed under his gaze, wishing he wouldn't look as though he wanted to devour her. Wasn't he taking the act a little too far? 'They've given me a weekly slot on Monday evenings at seven o'clock. Caroline designed a poster for me on the computer this morning and I've got some handouts for people.'

She'd been surprised and relieved when Caroline had suggested working on a poster. After a few days off, the woman had seemed almost cheerful. Holly hoped that it was the start of a more comfortable working relationship.

'What sort of class will you do?' Samantha looked at her with interest and Holly smiled.

'Well, basically it will be a general keep-fit session, suitable for everyone.'

'Maybe I'll come.' Samantha flexed her muscles and did a little dance. 'The only exercise I get is chewing lettuce leaves.'

'Typical dietician.' Mark rolled his eyes and gave her a crooked grin. 'Why can't you battle with saturated fat like the rest of the population?'

'Probably because I'm a "typical dietician",' Samantha said tartly, 'and, anyway, you're a fine one to talk! You're hardly out of shape yourself, Mark.'

They all glanced at Mark except Holly who studiously looked the other way. She was becoming a bit too conscious of just how good Mark's body was and she didn't want to think about it any more than necessary.

'OK, folks.' Ian glanced at his watch. 'Let's open the doors.'

After that there was a steady stream of people and Holly was kept busy checking blood pressures and talking about the importance of diet and exercise.

'I've smoked forty a day since I was eighteen,' one man told her gloomily, holding out his arm for the blood pressure check. 'I know I need to stop, but I just can't kick the habit.'

Holly checked his blood pressure and recorded it carefully. 'It's very hard, Mr Finn,' she said quietly. 'It's an addiction, and if it was that easy to give up, everyone would have done so a long time ago. We need to try and find a way that will work for you.'

'I'm full of good intentions and I've stopped quite a few times,' he admitted, rubbing his craggy face with nicotine-stained fingers. 'But I always start again.'

'That's often what happens when people try and battle with an addiction,' Holly assured him. 'Look on it as part of the giving up process. Modifying addictive behaviour isn't easy. The important thing is that you keep trying! What makes you start again, do you know?'

'Not really.' He shrugged. 'The first time I went to the pub and everyone else was smoking and that was that. The second time it was my daughter's wedding and the wife was so stressed out I was desperate for a cigarette.'

'What's the longest time that you've given up for?'

'Three months,' he told her, and then gave a rueful grin. 'And that was after my heart attack. I was too ill to lift a cigarette.'

Holly smiled but her eyes were serious. 'You know how important it is to give up, don't you, Mr Finn?'

'Yeah.' He nodded slowly. 'Dr Logan reads me the Riot Act every time I see him. Says that people like me who smoke after a heart attack double their risk of dying.'

'And he's right, you know that.' Holly's voice was gentle and Mr Finn pulled a face.

'Yeah—and this time I'm determined to stick at it.'

'Good for you.' Holly sat back in her chair and looked

at him thoughtfully. 'So we need to persevere and find a method that helps you give up.'

She spent a long time with Mr Finn, talking about his lifestyle, trying to look for solutions together to solve his smoking problem, then she sent him to see Mark with a request for nicotine replacement.

'How did you do with Mr Finn?' Ian asked her as they stopped for a five-minute break between patients.

'Quite well, I think.' Holly frowned. 'We decided that his lifestyle encouraged his smoking, so he's going to give some thought to taking up a hobby of some sort to stop him going to the pub on a Friday night. And he's going to see Mark for nicotine replacement.'

'If you can stop Jack Finn going to the pub on a Friday night then you're a genius,' Mark drawled as he passed on his way to see Samantha. 'I've given him a prescription for nicotine replacement but I'm not overly optimistic. He's never come back two weeks running before.'

Holly smiled broadly. 'He's promised to come back next week and he's signed up for my exercise class.'

Mark stopped in his tracks. 'He's signed up for your *exercise class*?'

'Absolutely.' Holly laughed at the look on his face and her eyes challenged him. 'Why shouldn't he?'

'Well, because…' Mark gave a gulp of disbelief and shook his head. 'Because keep fit isn't exactly Jack Finn's scene. I can't see him in Lycra somehow, can you, Ian?'

Ian was laughing. 'Frankly, no. How did you do it, Holly?'

'You're both awful!' Holly gave them a disapproving look. 'For a start, keeping fit isn't about Lycra and it certainly isn't restricted to women. How about you, Mark? You keep fit, what's the difference?'

Mark was still laughing, undaunted by her disapproval. 'That's different. I don't dance around a room in tights.'

'Which just goes to show that you've never attended one of my classes,' Holly said calmly. 'I challenge you to join us on Monday, Dr Logan. You might be surprised. In fact, that's an excellent idea. If I can tell everyone that you'll be there, too, it will encourage the rest of the men.'

'Great idea!' Ian slapped Mark on the shoulders and Mark shook his head, his gorgeous eyes still creased with laughter.

'I'm not much of a dancer, Holl.'

'It isn't about dancing,' Holly told him primly. 'It's about keeping fit. And seeing as you pride yourself on being in peak condition, you can come and show us all how it's done. I'll guarantee you'll sweat.'

'Yes, boss.' Mark grinned at her and she smiled back, admitting to herself that he was a good sport.

'And, for your information, I haven't called it Keep Fit.' She reached across to one of the tables and picked up a leaflet that Caroline had designed for her that morning. 'Caroline and I decided that Get Physical had more of a universal appeal. It's going to be a series of eight classes to begin with and I'm going to give everyone additional exercises to do in between classes at home.'

'Are you really hoping to attract lots of men?' Samantha asked curiously. 'I think that's a brilliant idea. The men always get left out.'

'If Holly's dressed in Lycra the men will be queuing back to Dorset,' Mark said dryly, touching her gently on the cheek. 'Better wear a baggy tracksuit.'

Holly rolled her eyes and gave him a disapproving look. 'Haven't you got anything better to do than laugh at my fitness class?'

Mark grinned. 'Offhand I can't think of anything—'

'Come on, lad.' Ian grabbed him by the arm. 'Mrs Fry has just come in and you know you're her favourite.'

Mark groaned and followed Ian across the room, leaving Holly with Samantha.

'I've gathered a group of eight in the coffee-room,' Samantha told her, handing her a list of names. 'Mostly women, all wanting to discuss diets. We're ready when you are.'

'Brilliant.' Holly gave her a smile. 'Let's get started, then, shall we?'

The two women sat down with the group and amazingly quickly everyone was talking freely about their dietary habits and worries.

'It's just so complicated,' one woman moaned as she looked at the diet sheet. 'I know you're meant to eat more fish, but which fish?'

'Oily fish is good,' Samantha told her. 'Things like mackerel, sardines, salmon.'

'I know what I'm meant to eat,' another woman said, 'but I haven't got the time to cook one thing for me and another for the family.'

'So we need to find recipes that are low in fat and suitable for you,' Holly said quickly, 'but still appealing to the family.'

'But they don't want to lose weight,' someone protested, and Samantha nodded.

'That's true, but almost everyone could do with cutting the amount of saturated fat that they eat, so what you need to do is plan a healthy menu and just give them larger portions. They can eat more potatoes and more pasta and fill up on vegetables.'

'How do I stop eating chocolate?' someone asked. And some of the other women chipped in with ideas and suggestions to help.

By the end of the session all the women were firm friends and agreed that sharing their problems had somehow made it all more interesting.

'Will you be doing this again next week?' one of them asked as they were leaving, and Samantha nodded.

'Definitely, if you'd like to. Why not all choose a recipe that your family has enjoyed and then we can share them around?'

There was a murmur of agreement and the group left the room, chatting.

'Ready to go home?' Mark was waiting for her in the corridor, his car keys in his hand. 'Tina and Ian are locking up this week. Our turn next week.'

They said goodnight to the rest of the team and walked out towards the car park.

'How on earth did you persuade Caroline to help you with your posters?' Mark looked at her curiously as he held the door open for her to pass through. 'I thought she was being less than helpful before?'

Holly gave a shrug. 'She just offered. I don't know why. Ever since her days off she's been more cheerful. She was being really nice to me this morning.'

'Hmm.' Mark fiddled with his car keys as they strolled across the car park. 'I noticed her talking to Greg earlier in the week. I wonder—'

Raucous laughter interrupted him and Holly froze as she saw a group of teenage boys drinking and misbehaving in the street outside the medical centre.

Realising that she'd stopped walking, Mark paused and glanced back at her, his eyes narrowing.

'Holl?' He closed the distance between them and frowned down at her. 'What's wrong?'

'Nothing.' She was being ridiculous, but she couldn't help it. It took so little for it all to come rushing back. In this case it was the sound of laughter. Totally innocent laughter, but it just reminded her…

Instinctively she moved closer to Mark and he slipped an arm round her shoulders in a protective gesture.

'How long is it going to take you to tell me about this?' His voice was grim and his arm clamped her firmly against him.

For a brief moment she allowed herself to enjoy the safety of his arms and then she pulled away.

'There's nothing to tell, Mark,' she said, her voice firm. 'I'm fine now. I was just a bit…cold.'

'Cold.' He stared at her for a long moment, jangling the keys in his long fingers as his eyes searched hers. 'Right. We'll leave it at that for now. But sooner or later you are going to have to tell me what's going on and it had better be sooner, Holly.'

She was drinking coffee on the deck the next morning when Mark joined her, his dark hair still damp from the shower.

'You're looking smart for a Saturday,' he said on seeing her tailored skirt and neat blouse.

'I'm going to see Anna Watts,' Holly told him, finishing her coffee and putting the mug down on the table. 'She was so desperate when we saw her on Thursday. I don't want to leave it until next week.'

Mark sighed. 'Holly—'

'She's on her own, Mark,' Holly said firmly. 'Her husband is never there and she has no support. I just want to talk to her and teach her a few basic massage techniques. If we can stop the baby crying it might ease her stress levels.'

There was a brief silence and then Mark gave her a smile. 'OK. Fine. Give me five minutes and I'll come with you.'

Holly's eyes widened. 'You?'

'Why not me?' He turned and walked back to the kitchen, making himself a coffee and dropping two slices of bread into the toaster. 'She's my patient, too, remember? And besides, I'd like to see how she's doing.'

Less than an hour later they pulled up outside Anna's tiny cottage, and before they even left the car they could hear the baby screaming.

Mark frowned. 'That baby does *not* sound happy.'

Holly nodded. 'No wonder Anna's in a state.'

'No wonder,' he agreed, his mouth set in a grim line. 'Looks like you were right to visit.'

They knocked on the door and Anna finally opened the door, still in her dressing-gown. Her hair fell limp and straggly over her thin shoulders.

She looked pale and very, very tired.

'Oh, Dr Logan.' She looked flustered and wrapped her dressing gown more tightly around her waist. 'I wasn't expecting—I mean—'

'Can we come in, Anna?' Mark asked gently. 'Sister Foster promised to teach you some massage techniques and I thought I'd come, too, and see how you were.'

'Oh.' Anna looked embarrassed and self-conscious. 'I'm really sorry I'm not dressed yet. I don't know where the morning's gone. I'll put the kettle on for you.'

'Don't worry about not being dressed.' Mark was quick to put her at ease. 'My sister, who has a set of twins, tells me that she's gone through an entire day without getting dressed before now, so you don't need to explain.'

'And don't worry about the kettle either,' Holly said firmly, sliding past Mark and giving the woman a warm smile. 'Let's have a look at Harry and see why he's crying.'

Anna bit her lip and walked towards the screaming. 'He does that for most of the day,' she told them, pushing open the sitting-room door. 'I think that's why my husband is out so much at the moment. He just can't stand the noise. Actually I don't really blame him.'

Holly bent over the Moses basket which had been placed on the sofa. 'What's the matter with you, little fellow? Have you got a tummyache or is it something more?'

'Why don't I take a good look at him, Anna?' Mark suggested, putting his bag down on the floor and giving her a smile. 'If there seems to be nothing wrong, we can take it from there. Has he been like this since his immunisations?'

Anna shook her head. 'Oh, no. He's been like this since I brought him home from hospital.'

'He had a very traumatic start to life,' Mark said, undressing the baby deftly and examining him with careful hands. 'And some babies just cry more than others, I'm afraid. It may just be that. How's he feeding?'

'Fine.' Anna watched anxiously.

'And he isn't sick after feeds?'

'No. Debra weighed him for me at clinic yesterday and he's growing nicely.'

Mark rummaged in his bag for a paediatric stethoscope and listened to the baby's heart and lungs.

'Physically everything seems fine, Anna,' he said finally, looping the stethoscope round his neck and lifting the screaming bundle carefully. 'Come and have a cuddle with your Uncle Mark and tell me what's wrong.'

Holly felt her stomach flip as she watched him with the baby, his large hands stroking the tiny frame until the screams subsided.

'He does like to be held, but I can't carry him around all day,' Anna said helplessly. 'I don't know what to do about it.'

'My sister had a sling,' Mark said, transferring the baby to his other shoulder. 'That way she could carry one of the twins everywhere she went.'

Anna bit her lip. 'I haven't tried that.'

'Have you got one?' Holly asked, and Anna nodded.

'Yes. You know what it's like with your first. You get given piles of things. There's one upstairs under the bed.'

'Why don't you go and find it and, in the meantime,

we'll undress Harry and see if he likes massage,' Holly suggested, delving in her bag for some oil.

'What's that?' Mark laid the baby down gently on the sofa and watched while she undid the poppers of his blue sleepsuit.

'Almond oil.' Holly rubbed the oil into her palms to smooth and warm them just as Anna returned. 'I'm just about to start, Anna. Can you take off his vest for me, please?'

Anna slipped off the vest and Holly gently massaged the tiny body, moving her hands gently and slowly down in soothing waves. At first Harry seemed a bit fretful, but then he seemed to settle down.

'He's enjoying it,' Anna whispered in amazement. 'Look at his little face.'

'Yes, he's relaxed now,' Holly agreed. 'You're right that his tummy was very tense. I think that might well have been the problem.'

'Oh, it's bliss not to hear him screaming,' Anna breathed. 'Can I do it?'

'Of course.' Holly moved to one side. 'Just rub some oil into your palms. That's it. Now, very gently just move your hands… That's it… Perfect…'

Together they stroked the baby and with each touch Anna's spirits seemed to lift.

By the time Mark and Holly climbed back into the car, Anna was looking relaxed and almost cheerful.

'Phone me if there's a crisis,' Holly instructed, 'otherwise see Debra in clinic next week. Please?'

'I promise I'll go,' Anna said with a shy smile. 'And thank you.'

As they drove off Mark grinned at her. 'I didn't know you were such a dab hand at massage. I've got this terrible pain in my stomach. I don't suppose you'd—?'

'No, you're right,' Holly replied with a reproving look,

'I definitely wouldn't. You're much too big and ugly. I only do babies.'

'I'm a baby,' Mark said firmly. 'You should see me with spiders.'

'You, Mark Logan, aren't afraid of anything,' Holly said dryly, and he gave her broad smile and a wink.

'Oh, well, you can't blame a chap for trying.' He swung the car into the drive and pulled on the handbrake. 'How about tomorrow during our kiss? Maybe some massage would work then. What do you think?'

For a brief moment Holly's eyes dropped to his firm mouth and she wondered what it would be like to be kissed by a man like Mark.

She swallowed hard. She was going crazy!

'What I think is that you've gone nuts! We do *not* need to kiss each other to prove that we're together,' she said hastily, climbing out of the car quickly to try and escape the strange feelings that were swamping her. 'I promise to look at you adoringly. That should be fine.'

Mark slammed the door and walked round the car towards her. 'Don't be a spoilsport. I've been planning this great romantic scenario…'

Holly ignored him and hurried towards the front door. The more she thought about it, the more she was dreading this barbecue. She only hoped he was joking about the kiss.

'Smugglers' Bay', as it was called by the locals, was easily reached by a narrow coast road which ended in a tiny car park right next to the beach.

It was the perfect spot for a beach barbecue and Holly soon discovered that the event had been planned like a military operation, with each practice taking responsibility for a different aspect of the evening. Her practice had provided all the drinks and Ian and Mark were busy unloading crates of various beverages and mixing a punch.

The bay was beautiful, a perfect curve of yellow sand with rock pools and caves and a steep cliff path that rose away from the tiny car park.

Holly was staring at the yachts bobbing in the evening sunshine when Mark called her.

'Come and meet Greg, my sailing partner.' He waved a hand in her direction. 'And taste my punch.'

Dutifully she walked across to where he was standing, wondering whether she should have dressed up a bit more. She'd chosen to wear a pair of white shorts teamed with her favourite black sleeveless T-shirt. It was perfect for a warm evening, although hardly formal. But, then, Mark wasn't dressed formally either. He'd thrown on a pair of khaki shorts and a white T-shirt that clung to the powerful muscles of his shoulders. Despite his casual dress, he looked overwhelmingly handsome and Holly had noticed several of the women casting surreptitious looks in his direction.

She felt a rush of annoyance. The man was supposed to be engaged, for goodness' sake! No wonder Mark had problems—women couldn't seem to leave him alone!

'Hello, there.' She smiled at the good-looking blonde man standing by Mark's side and he narrowed his eyes and nodded slowly.

'Well, now everything is clear.'

Holly looked blank. 'I don't understand—what's clear?'

'The reason Mark was looking so stressed and now seems so relaxed.' Greg shot Mark a sly grin. 'If I'd been separated from a woman like this one, I would have been depressed, too.'

Holly blushed, feeling like a total fraud, but Mark just laughed and pulled her into his arms, giving her a huge hug.

'Absolutely. She's gorgeous, isn't she?' He smiled into her eyes and for a wild moment she thought that he was going to give her the kiss that he'd been threatening, but he released her, turning back to Greg with an easy smile. 'So, how are you getting on with Caroline? I saw you talking to her the other day.'

'Mark!' Holly was aghast. 'Stop interfering with other people's love lives.'

Mark grinned and stirred the punch. 'Just call me Cupid.'

'I could think of a less flattering name,' Greg said mildly, bending down and extracting a beer from the cool-bag. 'And I hardly need to remind you that Caroline and I were getting on nicely until you arrived on the scene.'

Mark cleared his throat and looked embarrassed. 'I'm sorry. It wasn't exactly my fault—'

'I know that.' Greg gave a wry smile and a fatalistic shrug. 'Which is why I'm drinking this beer and not pouring it down your neck. And the answer to your question is, yes, I was talking to her the other day. The truth is she's still pretty upset about you and Holly. I suppose she feels rejected again, but I'm gently reminding her that you never had a relationship in the first place.'

'Thanks, Greg. I owe you.' Mark gave him a brief smile and Holly leaned forward and helped herself to a small glass of punch.

'Don't you *mind* that she has a crush on Mark?'

'Holly, every female round here has a crush on Mark,' Greg said calmly, taking a gulp of beer and squinting slightly into the evening sun. 'You're probably the one that ought to mind.'

Holly shrugged and smiled. 'I'm used to it,' she said honestly. 'Girls have been attacking him since we were in primary school together. Nothing's changed.'

'I can well believe it.' Greg finished his beer and tossed the can into the bin. 'Anyway, I think Caroline is getting over it. She realises that everything was just in her head. Pass me another beer, Mark.'

Mark frowned. 'Why are you drinking beer instead of my punch?'

'Because I've seen what you've put in that punch,' Greg drawled, his blue eyes gleaming, 'and I need to be able to walk home in a straight line later. I've got my reputation to think of.'

There was general laughter and soon the evening was filled with delicious smells from the barbecue, friendly chatter and light music.

Holly tucked into barbecued chicken wings and hot sweetcorn dripping with melted butter.

'You've got butter on your chin.' Mark chuckled softly and wiped her face with a napkin. 'How's that punch? Need a top-up?'

Holly shook her head. 'No way! If I drink any more I won't be able to stand! Now I know why Greg chose the lager.'

A little distance away she could see Caroline watching them and suddenly her appetite vanished.

'What's wrong?' Mark frowned down at her and then nodded grimly. 'On second thoughts, don't tell me. I can guess. She's watching us, isn't she?'

'Mark—'

'Come on, let's go for a walk.' Without waiting for her answer, he took her plate and deposited it on a trestle table then slipped an arm round her shoulders, guiding her further onto the beach.

'Where are we going?' Knowing that people were watching them, Holly felt her face heat.

'For a walk. And some privacy.' His eyes were amused. 'Why are you embarrassed? This is a social gathering, not work. We're engaged. We're supposed to want to be alone together.'

Alone together. Her insides suddenly squirmed in a strange fashion. She'd been alone with Mark on countless occasions, but suddenly when he said it like that it seemed intimate and personal. Being alone with Mark as her 'lover' didn't seem the same as being alone with Mark as her friend.

They walked to the first cave and peered inside, avoiding the drips that fell from the roof at regular intervals.

'How far back do you think it goes?' Holly murmured, peering into the darkness towards the back of the cave.

'Goodness knows, and I don't intend to find out.' Mark reached up and touched the damp, jagged rocks. 'The tide's on the way in and these caves fill up at high tide.'

Holly gazed at the sea and shuddered. 'Awful to be trapped. Just imagine…'

'I'd rather not if you don't mind. Oops.' His voice was soft, his handsome face shadowed by the cave. 'We're under observation. Caroline's followed us. Time for some serious canoodling, I think.'

'Don't be ridiculous! We can't!' Holly's heart stumbled in her chest. Serious canoodling? What exactly did he have in mind?

His eyes dropped to her mouth and for endless seconds he studied her, his breathing steady and even. Holly stood frozen to the spot, her brain refusing to function, her thought processes jammed by the sudden tension between them.

And then he lowered his head slowly, almost hesitantly, as if he wasn't totally committed to what he was doing, wasn't totally convinced that it was right, despite his carefree attitude. When their mouths were separated by only a breath he paused and she felt a sharp current shoot through her lower body, leaving her limbs trembling and weak. Dear God, what was the matter with her? He hadn't even touched her yet. It was just the anticipation…

And then he did touch her. Softly at first, his mouth tasted hers. Gently. So gently. Teasing and coaxing a response from her. He held her firmly and his kiss was a carefully controlled, purposeful seduction designed to make her knees tremble and her insides spark. His mouth moved on hers with the sure, confident touch of a man who knew exactly how to kiss a woman, and it was nothing like any kiss Holly had ever had before. It was perfect. Absolutely perfect. Until it stopped.

He lifted his head suddenly and stared down at her, an odd expression in his dark eyes as they locked with hers.

Her heart thumping, Holly found her voice. 'Has she gone?'

'Gone?' For a moment he looked blank and then his eyes flicked up briefly and he glanced over her shoulder.

'Mark?'

Why wasn't he saying anything? 'Is she still watching?'

He seemed to hesitate for a brief second and then, without giving her an answer, his head came down and he kissed her again.

Only this time it was different.

This time, instead of a carefully orchestrated seduction, it was as if he couldn't help himself. He kissed her as if she was a temptation that he couldn't resist, his kiss rough and dominating, possessively male, arousing a storm of sensation which made her gasp against his mouth and curl her slim fingers into the front of his shirt for support.

How could a kiss feel like this? Like an explosion of fireworks inside her body, like an electric shock that shook every one of her senses?

As if acknowledging her need, his arm tightened protectively and his free hand slid into her hair and tilted her face, giving him better access to her mouth. This close, she was aware of every inch of him, aware of his hard thighs pressed against her softer ones, aware of his strength as he held her, aware of her thudding heart and her trembling limbs.

Oblivious to everything except the way he made her feel, she gave a tiny moan and wound her arms round his strong neck, feeling his hair brushing her fingertips. Lost in a swirling mist of desire, Holly gave in to the demands of his mouth, totally unable to do anything but respond. For the first time in her life she knew what it was like to be thoroughly kissed, and the experience left her weak and shaking.

When he finally lifted his head, she clutched at him dizzily, her breathing uneven.

'I gather she was still watching.' Her voice was husky and decidedly unsteady and she blushed furiously, hoping he wouldn't notice just how much his touch had affected her.

'Watching…?' He took a deep breath and glanced over her shoulder, his expression unreadable. 'Oh…yes.'

She swallowed, wondering when he was going to let her go. His strong arms still held her firmly against the solid muscle of his chest as if he was reluctant to release her. Which could only mean that Caroline was still there.

'Has she gone?' Standing in the protective circle of his arms felt so good—too good—but she knew it couldn't last. That it wasn't real. 'Mark?'

'What?' He stared down at her and his eyes locked with hers for endless seconds. Then he released her. 'Yes, she's gone. Greg dragged her away. She looked pretty upset.'

Mark's voice sounded oddly strained and he strode to the edge of the cave, his back towards her, his broad shoulders tense.

Without his arms around her Holly suddenly felt lost and confused. What was she meant to say after a kiss like that? What was she meant to do? Was she really expected to act as if nothing had happened? As if what they'd shared was common practice between good friends?

But Mark didn't seem bothered—it seemed that all he could think about was Caroline, and whether their ruse had worked.

Holly stared past him, frowning slightly as she realised that there was no longer anyone on the beach. They must have walked away very quickly.

She closed her eyes briefly and wondered whether her heart rate was ever going to return to normal. Hadn't Mark felt it, too? That overwhelming electricity that had burned through her entire body? No, obviously not, she thought miserably, or he wouldn't have released her so quickly and wouldn't be ignoring her now. To Mark it had just been a kiss. A kiss like any other. And she knew better than most just how many other women he'd kissed in his life.

Well, all that practice had certainly paid dividends. He was a good kisser. Lifting a hand, she brushed blonde hair away from her face and touched her lips with shaking fingers, remembering how it had felt when he'd touched her. Not just good. *Incredible.* Mark was an incredible kisser.

Breathing steadily to slow down her heart rate, she walked past him to the mouth of the cave, hoping that he wouldn't notice that her legs were shaking.

Mark.

Dear God, this was Mark. *Her Mark.* He was her oldest and dearest friend and yet—and yet at the moment when he'd kissed her he hadn't felt like a friend at all. He'd felt like a lover.

Only he wasn't her lover and never would be. He'd just kissed her for the benefit of observers. It hadn't been special to Mark.

But it had been special to her...

'Well, that should have convinced her,' Mark murmured as he stared across the beach. 'We'd better be getting back, I suppose.'

His voice was calm and relaxed, giving no hint that anything had changed for him. Which it hadn't, of course. He'd been thinking about Caroline all the time. Acting out a part.

Unlike her. She hadn't been acting. For Holly it had been all too real.

She'd kissed her best friend and suddenly everything that had been so clear was now confused.

# CHAPTER FIVE

WHAT was she going to say to Mark?

A sleepless night had done nothing to clear Holly's head, nothing at all. And now she had to face him. She swallowed hard and paused at the bottom of the staircase, trying to pretend that the kiss they'd shared had meant nothing to her. That their relationship was exactly the same as it had always been.

But it wasn't the same and she knew that it never would be again…

Taking a deep breath, she pushed open the kitchen door, smiling brightly at Mark who was lounging at the kitchen table, reading a newspaper.

'Any coffee going?' Avoiding his eyes, she walked briskly across to the coffee-machine.

'Good morning.' Mark sounded incredibly normal and she forced herself to turn and face him.

She had to act naturally, as if her world hadn't really been turned upside down.

'Good morning.' The words almost stuck in her throat as she noticed how handsome he looked first thing in the morning, his jaw dark and rough and his loose T-shirt doing nothing to disguise the powerful muscle of his chest and shoulders. Suddenly finding it difficult to breathe, Holly vowed not to make an appearance before he was fully dressed on future occasions. Her knees trembling, she turned back to the coffee-machine and paid it rather more attention than it needed.

'So, what are your plans for today?' Mark leaned back

in his chair and pushed the newspaper to one side, running long fingers through his cropped dark hair.

'Plans?' She was going to spend the day trying to persuade herself that nothing had changed. That she didn't really find him attractive. Those were her plans.

'I thought you might fancy a walk.' Mark poured milk over a bowl of cereal and picked up a spoon, totally calm and relaxed. Clearly he wasn't suffering the same inner torment that she was. 'The coast path from here leads down to some fantastic rocky bays. We could take a picnic and go for a swim.'

*Spend the day with him?*

It was clear that, for him at least, nothing had changed, and Holly nibbled her lip, trying to subdue a flash of disappointment. What had she expected? That he'd fall down on one knee and confess that he'd always loved her? Ridiculous!

So now what was she going to do? On the one hand, a day with Mark sounded like heaven, but on the other, could she actually be with him all day and act normally? Could she spend time with him without staring, without remembering—

Oh, for goodness' sake! She took a deep breath and pulled herself together. She had to get on with her life. Mark wasn't responsible for the way she felt—she was. She'd let it all get to her. Nothing had changed. Not really. He was still the same Mark she'd always known. OK, so he was a good kisser—or, to be more accurate, he was an exceptional kisser—but just because he knew how to kiss a woman senseless, that didn't mean that their friendship was affected. She was being pathetic.

'I'd love to go for a walk,' she said firmly, lifting her small chin and giving him the brightest smile she could manage. 'I'll just grab some breakfast and then I'll change.'

They gathered together a picnic and set off from the

house, following the coastal path along the edge of the cliff and down towards a rocky bay.

Holly walked steadily, her gaze fixed on the sea and the rocks. It was either that or give in to the compulsion to look at Mark who was striding ahead of her, a rucksack on his broad shoulders, long muscular legs eating up the ground with ease. And if she looked, she'd dream. And dreaming was no way to sort out the tangled mess inside her head.

At a curve in the path he paused, watching the antics of two boats in the bay.

'What on earth are they doing?' Mark frowned, his eyes narrowing as he watched the two boats dropping anchor and heard the sound of raucous male laughter. 'The currents here are deadly so I hope they're not planning to swim off the boat—especially after drinking. Alcohol and water are a pretty lethal combination.'

'It's a pretty cove,' Holly murmured, lifting a hand to shield her eyes from the sun as she followed the direction of his gaze. 'It doesn't look that dangerous.'

'Don't you believe it,' Mark said grimly, his firm mouth unsmiling as he watched the horseplay on the yacht. 'The current is strong, the rocks are vicious and the water is freezing.'

Holly bit her lip. She'd forgotten how well he knew this area. 'Should we warn them?'

Mark shook his head. 'Technically they're not doing anything wrong so it's really none of our business and, anyway, they're too far away to hear us.' He stared at the boats for another moment and then gave a small shrug. 'Come on, I want to show you the view further on. You can usually see seals and basking sharks from the top of that hill.'

By the time they reached the top of the hill they were both out of breath.

'It's fantastic!' Holly stared across the bay, wishing she weren't quite so conscious of his every movement. He'd dropped his powerful length onto the grass and closed his eyes as if nothing in the world troubled him. Oh, bother, bother, bother! Nothing was *ever* going to be the same again. Instead of Mark the friend, suddenly all she could see was Mark the man. And what a man...

She stifled a groan, fighting her own thoughts.

Why had she never noticed the powerful swell of muscle underneath his shirt or just how strong and muscular his legs were? She must have been blind.

His voice cut through her thoughts, deep and very male. 'See any sharks?'

'Sharks?' Holly cleared her throat. She hadn't given the sharks a thought. Hiding her blush, she delved into his rucksack for the binoculars. 'No. But I don't really know what I'm looking for.'

'A fin.' Mark propped himself up on his elbows, openly laughing at her. 'You've seen *Jaws*, haven't you?'

'I never believe what I see at the movies,' Holly mumbled, horribly flustered by him. She held the binoculars to her face, relieved to have a reason to look away from him. 'I don't see anything. Just sea.'

'Useless woman—here, let me.' Mark sat up and took the binoculars from her, his fingers brushing hers and sending a current of electricity running through her body.

He squinted through the binoculars and, safe from detection, she treated herself to a brief look at his profile, her eyes drifting hungrily over the hard ridge of his cheekbones and resting on his rough jaw. Obviously he hadn't bothered to shave that morning and the dark stubble made him look wickedly sexy. Just looking at his firm, well-shaped mouth made her stomach tumble as she remembered every tingle and thrill that had run through her body when he'd kissed her. He was breathtakingly good-looking and for the first time in her life she was beginning to understand why women behaved so stupidly around Mark.

In fact, if she didn't rapidly pull herself together, she was going to be joining all those silly females she'd laughed at over the years.

And it was all because of one kiss.

Just one kiss was all it had taken to open her eyes...

'Nope—can't see any. I've brought you up here under false pretences.' He lowered the binoculars and turned, his grin fading as he caught her studying him. 'Holly?'

His dark eyes narrowed questioningly and she swallowed hard.

Oh, help! She'd been looking like a dreamy female, she knew she had!

'I thought I saw an insect on your neck,' she mumbled, blushing deeply as she scrambled hastily to her feet and swept her long blonde hair away from her face. 'Let's find somewhere for a picnic, shall we? I'm starving.'

'An *insect*?' He repeated her words with gentle emphasis and for a moment his gaze was searching. Then he rose to his feet in a fluid movement and dragged his eyes away from her.

'That's usually fairly private.' He gestured towards another little cove. 'We could eat there and have a swim if you fancied it.'

Without waiting for her reply, he set off down the path and she stared after him, her heart thumping. Private. The cove was private? She would have preferred a bustling harbour with plenty of people to take her mind off Mark. Private was just going to make things worse.

With a resigned sigh she forced herself to walk after him. He'd only kissed her once, for goodness' sake! What on earth was the matter with her? What was it about one kiss that had turned her into a gibbering, mooning wreck? Why was she behaving like some teenager with a giant crush?

Still trying to talk sense into herself, she followed him down the path, stifling a groan as she saw him swing the rucksack off his back and strip down to his swimming shorts.

Anyone would think he was doing it on purpose to torment her, she thought, gritting her teeth and averting her eyes. It was bad enough trying not to notice Mark's incredible physique when he was fully clothed, but when he stripped off…

Despite her best efforts her eyes slid back to him and goose-bumps prickled her skin as she stared at his broad, muscular shoulders and strong legs. Muttering under her breath, she quickly dipped her head and dropped onto the grass, staring intently at the sea. The sea. Cold. Wet. Apparently full of basking sharks. Surely if she concentrated hard enough on the sea, she'd be able to forget about Mark's body.

'Coming for a swim?'

He strolled up to her and hunkered down in front of her, his very bare chest only inches away from her eyes. She suppressed a whimper. Great. So much for avoiding him. How could he be so relaxed with her? But, then, why shouldn't he be relaxed? Mark thought she was immune to him…

'A swim? In a minute maybe,' she said weakly, turning aside and rummaging in the rucksack. 'You go ahead. I need a drink.' Preferably an alcoholic one to numb her senses.

Mark watched her closely and for a moment she thought she saw a flicker of amusement in those dark eyes, and then he gave a shrug of those broad shoulders and straightened before sprinting towards the sea, leaving her sitting on the grass in a state of total confusion.

\*    \*    \*

It was late afternoon by the time they started back along the cliff path and by then Holly had her emotions well in hand again.

Just Mark, just Mark, just Mark, she recited steadily as she plodded back up the cliff behind him, her eyes fixed firmly on the rough ground.

As they reached the path above the rocky bay Holly noticed a small group of people gathering and pointing. She frowned and screwed up her eyes against the sun. There was something about the way they were standing, looking out to sea—something that wasn't quite right—

'Something's wrong Mark—look!' She put a hand on his arm, feeling the hard muscle under her fingers.

Mark glanced at the group of people and then out to the bay, swearing softly as he saw what they were looking at. 'One of those boys is in the water. Damn it, I knew there was going to be trouble.'

He shook off her restraining hand and sprinted up to the group gathered on the path.

'What's happening?' He barked the question at the nearest man, who shook his head briefly.

'Nothing good, mate. They've all been drinking—we've been watching them for most of the afternoon while we were having our picnic. They were larking around and then one of the lads dived in, fully clothed, and he hasn't come up again. They've been trying to look for him but the tide's coming in and the waves are too rough.'

Mark stared at him. 'How long has he been in the water?'

'About five minutes.'

Mark's lips tightened. 'Has anyone called the lifeboat?'

'Lifeboat?' The man shook his head again, looking helpless. 'No, there's no phone—one of us has run back to the village but it's at least half an hour away.'

'Holly, there's a mobile in my rucksack,' Mark's voice was sharp. 'Call the coastguard and an ambulance. Then get yourself down that path and wait on the rocks. I'm going to need your help.'

'Mark, wait! You can't—'

But Mark had gone and Holly bit her lip, watching as he sprinted up the path, away from the cove. She frowned slightly. Why was he going that way? What was he doing?

And then she saw it.

A lifebelt and a rope, attached to a post to one side of the path.

Mark grabbed both and returned, jerking his head towards two of the men. 'I need someone to hold a rope.'

His intention was obvious and Holly felt a rush of panic.

'Mark, no!' Holly reached out to stop him but he shook her off easily, his eyes steely with determination.

'The phone, Holl!'

Holly watched helplessly as he ran down the path towards the rocks as fast as he safely could, the other men close behind him. She knew exactly what he was going to do. The same thing Mark always did when someone was in trouble. Take control. She closed her eyes briefly and faced reality. Mark was going to go into the water after the boy and there was nothing she could do to stop him.

But she could get him help.

Her hands shaking, she rummaged in his rucksack until she found his phone, switching it on and dialling with difficulty as she watched the three men descend to the craggy rocks at the bottom of the cove.

Despite her panic, her A and E training took over and she gave the details to the emergency services quickly and calmly before reaching into the rucksack to see what else Mark carried. Did he have a first aid kit? Yes. She dragged it out and tucked it under her arm. Probably not much use but still…

Stumbling slightly in her haste, she started down the path, aware that one of the women was close behind her.

'He's a brave one, your young man,' she said, and Holly felt her heart lurch. She didn't want Mark to be brave. She wanted him to be alive, and she knew how many people had drowned going into cold water to save someone.

But Mark was sensible and experienced, she told herself firmly, gasping as her feet slipped on the steep path. He'd been sailing and swimming almost all his life and he knew the rules. He wouldn't take risks. Would he?

As soon as she arrived at the rocks she could see that he was taking as few risks as possible, masterminding the rescue attempt with a cool confidence that made her relax slightly.

He'd attached the rope firmly to his waist and had made one of the other men responsible for holding the end so that he had an escape route if he got into difficulties himself.

The third man was busy following Mark's orders, yelling to the other teenagers on the yachts not to go into the water after their friend.

'No point in having to rescue more than one of them,' he muttered to Holly as she picked her way over the rocks to his side.

Holly watched, her heart in her mouth, as Mark waded into the water and started to swim, working his way towards the boat with a steady crawl, a powerful stroke that soon closed the distance between him and the boat.

'He's a bloody good swimmer,' one of the men muttered in awe, and Holly nodded, her heart thudding unevenly.

'He is a good swimmer,' she agreed in a husky voice, 'but it isn't always the swimming that counts. It's the current and the cold. The cold can kill.'

And with that awful thought in her head, she stared anxiously across the mounting waves, watching as Mark swam up to one of the boats, his head barely visible as he spoke to the boys who were hanging over the side.

And then he disappeared under the water.

Holly tensed as she watched, telling herself that he knew what he was doing, that he was still attached to a rope.

And then she saw him surface and take several breaths before diving down again.

Four times he repeated the dive and finally, when she thought she couldn't stand the tension any longer, he surfaced, holding the limp figure of the boy.

Gasping for breath, he tilted the boy's head and started to swim back to shore with him, his movements hampered and slowed by the extra load.

The man next to Holly gathered up the slack in the rope and frowned slightly. 'I wonder why he didn't take him onto the boat?'

'Vertical lift,' Holly murmured, her eyes never leaving Mark as he struggled back towards them. Her heart was pounding uncomfortably in her chest and her whole body felt limp with fear. If anything happened to Mark—

'What did you say?' The man standing next to her was looking confused and she shook herself.

'He doesn't want to lift him vertically. You should always keep immersion victims horizontal if possible.'

The man steadied himself on the rocks and glanced at her. 'And what happens if you don't?'

Holly's eyes were still on Mark as she delved in her brain for the answer. Why was it? She couldn't concentrate when she was this worried… She tried to remember what she'd learned in A and E. Circum rescue collapse or something— yes, that was it.

'You can get a catastrophic drop in arterial blood pressure,' she told him, never looking away from Mark, 'for lots of reasons. Hypothermia means that the heart muscle can't work as well, and if you lift the patient vertically then the effects of gravity tend to increase pooling of the blood

in the legs. There's more, I think, but that's all I can remember.'

That and the importance of warming a profoundly cold
patient.

She snapped into action and searched Mark's first-aid kit,
hoping, hoping—

'Yes!'

She dragged a small packet out of the bag with a crow
of triumph and the man looked at her.

'What's that?'

'A space blanket,' Holly muttered, ripping it open ready
to be used. 'That boy is going to need warming up. Has
anyone got any other spare clothing?'

'We've got towels,' someone said, and Holly nodded
swiftly.

'Put everything that you've got in this pile. The more
windproof and waterproof stuff the better.'

'But it's June. Surely it isn't that cold,' one of the women
murmured, and Holly pulled a face.

'It is in the sea. He'll be chilled to the bone.'

Seeing that Mark was near the rocks she scrambled down
to him, being careful not to slip.

'What do you want me to do?'

He ran a hand over his face to clear his vision of sea
water, his dark lashes clumped together and his handsome
face drawn and tired from the exertion.

'I need to get him out but, Holly…' He paused to catch
his breath, his voice slightly hoarse. 'We need to keep him
horizontal. That's very important.'

'I remember.' Holly gave him a brief nod to indicate that
she understood and turned to the men. 'Quickly, he needs
help to lift him out. Keep him flat. Flat, OK?'

Between them the men managed to lift the teenager out
of the water and lay him on a smooth rock away from
the waves.

'Did you phone for help?' Mark squatted down next to their patient, his expression grim.

Holly nodded. 'Coastguard and air ambulance on the way.'

Mark placed his fingers on the young man's neck, feeling for a carotid pulse. 'Come on, come on,' he muttered, glancing at his watch. 'Give me a pulse.'

'Shouldn't we be starting resuscitation?' someone murmured and Holly shook her head quickly.

'People who've been in the water can have a slow pulse that's very difficult to feel—it doesn't mean it isn't there.'

She knew as well as Mark that if they started CPR when the heart was still beating they could trigger a fatal arrhythmia.

She glanced at her watch. 'Fifty seconds, Mark,' she said softly, and his mouth tightened.

'Come on—give me a pulse, damn it!' He gave a low growl of frustration and shifted his fingers slightly.

Holly bit her lip and checked her watch again. 'Sixty seconds, Mark. We ought to—'

'He's got a pulse,' Mark interrupted her triumphantly, glancing up as the sound of a helicopter cut through the summer evening. 'And we've got some help. One of you…' He jerked his head to one of the men again. 'Can you sprint up that path and say we need a nasogastric tube to relieve gastric dilatation and equipment to set up an IV?'

The man repeated it back to be sure he'd got the right message and then set off at a steady jog to meet the paramedics.

Mark slipped a hand inside the teenager's shirt, frowning as he touched the skin under his armpit.

'He's cold as marble. Let's wrap him up, Holly.' He nodded his approval as she produced the space blanket from his first-aid kit and started to cover their patient. 'Leave me an arm—I need to get a line in. If I can find a vein, that is. His entire peripheral circulation's probably shut down in the cold.'

As the paramedics scrambled and slid their way to the bottom of the slope, the police arrived along with the coastguard.

'Everyone's here now the rescue bit's over,' one of the men observed dryly, standing aside as uniformed professionals suddenly surged all around them.

'Dr Logan!' One of the paramedics dropped to his knees next to the patient and nodded to Mark. 'Glad to see you here. What do you need?'

'Let's get a line in,' Mark grated, 'and I want to pass a nasogastric tube and get some of the water out of his stomach.'

'Do we need to check his core temperature?' The paramedic ripped open a venflon and Holly held the man's arm while Mark searched for a vein.

'Don't waste your time. I've felt him and I can tell you that he's hypothermic. His skin feels like marble.' Mark frowned down at the man's veins. 'Damn it, I can't see a vein. Try the other arm, Holl—quickly!'

Holly lifted the other arm and squeezed, searching for a vein, and then Mark gave a grunt of satisfaction.

'Bingo!' He jerked his head towards her. 'Can you squeeze? I don't want to lose it.'

She locked her fingers round the man's arm and watched while Mark flicked the vein, his handsome face still glistening with sea water.

Brushing water out of his eyes with one strong forearm, Mark took the venflon and paused for a fraction of a second, his face a mask of concentration as he felt for the vein again. Then he gritted his teeth and inserted the venflon with a sure movement.

'OK, I'm in.'

There was a palpable sigh of relief from the paramedics. 'What do you need, Doc?'

'Plasma expander,' Mark said quickly. 'I need to try and combat the hypotension.'

Within minutes the intravenous infusion was running and Mark judged that it was time to evacuate the patient.

'We need to keep him horizontal,' he instructed, and as he dried himself with a towel, he huddled with the police and paramedics to try and work out the best way.

By the time they finally slid the stretcher into the waiting helicopter, Holly found herself shaking with reaction.

'Are you OK?' Mark hesitated as he pulled his top back on before climbing into the helicopter after his patient. 'Can you find your way home?'

'Of course.' She gave him a smile and a little push. 'You go. I'll see you later.'

They stood well back while the helicopter took off, carefully transporting the casualty to the nearest hospital.

The police were talking to the coastguard who agreed to talk to the rest of the boys on the boats.

'We'll need some sort of statement from you,' the policeman said, walking across to Holly. 'Looks like Dr Logan saved the day.'

'He was a hero,' one of the men said gruffly, and his wife nodded.

'Lucky for them he was passing and that he's so fit. Not many people would have made it through that water and managed to rescue that lad.'

Holly managed a stiff smile and the policeman frowned.

'You look a bit shocked, love. Why don't you come with us and we'll get you a hot drink?'

Holly shook her head. 'No, honestly. I'll be fine. It's only a short walk home for me.'

'Well, then, I'll walk with you,' the policeman said firmly, and she found herself surprisingly relieved to have his company. It stopped her thinking about what would have happened if she'd lost Mark.

It was dark by the time Mark returned, the sound of his key in the lock breaking the silence in the house.

'Holly?'

There was a clatter as he dropped his keys on the table and walked into the darkened living room.

'Holl?' His voice was sharp with concern and he flicked on the lights. 'Why are you in the dark? What's going on? Are you all right?'

'I'm fine,' she lied, tucking her legs further underneath herself on the sofa.

She wasn't fine at all. She was confused by her own feelings, by the strength of her feelings for Mark. She'd always known she loved him, of course; he was her oldest and dearest friend. But until this afternoon she hadn't known that she loved him like *that*.

'So why are you sitting in the dark, babe?' His soft endearment made her stomach flip and she hugged her arms round her slim body to try and subdue the sensation.

'I—I just feel a bit shocked. Stupid, I know…'

If she was lucky he'd misinterpret her words and assume that the shock she was referring to was the near drowning of the teenage boy.

She was right. That was exactly what he did.

'They think he'll be all right,' Mark told her, sitting down next to her. 'He was in the water for about ten minutes so it could have been worse. And he's young and there were no signs of aspiration.'

'That's good.' Holly hugged her arms more tightly round her body to prevent herself from giving in to the temptation to throw herself at him and hold him close.

'They think he'll make a full recovery,' Mark said, his eyes fixed on her face. 'The police and the coastguard have

SARAH MORGAN                    103

read the Riot Act to his friends, so it should be a happy ending.'

'Good.' She gave him a smile that cost her dearly in terms of effort. Oh, she was pleased about the boy, of course she was. But every time she closed her eyes she saw Mark ploughing through the water, risking his life to save a boy that he didn't even know.

And the incident had shown her, without a shadow of a doubt, that the reason she'd never managed to find a man she was interested in was because she loved Mark.

She loved Mark and she always had.

# CHAPTER SIX

'IT'S THE *Evening Herald* on the phone for Mark,' Caroline said, walking into the staffroom with an apologetic smile. 'Sorry. I tried to tell them that you didn't want to talk to any more journalists, but they were insistent.'

'I bet they were,' Mark muttered darkly, his mouth tightening as he picked up the phone.

Only half listening as Mark gave a reluctant interview to the persistent reporter, Holly glanced curiously at Caroline, noticing that she was wearing more make-up than usual and looked decidedly more cheerful. Was it Greg?

'Haven't they got anything better to stick in their newspapers than a story about me having a dip in the sea on a June afternoon?' Mark said, replacing the receiver and returning to his half-eaten sandwich.

'Everyone loves a hero, Mark,' Caroline said brightly, carefully loading a tray with mugs of coffee for the reception staff. 'It's nice to read something cheerful in the papers for a change.'

As the door swung closed behind her, Mark frowned. 'Is it my imagination or was she wearing make-up?'

'She was definitely wearing make-up.' Holly cast him a dubious look. 'Do you think it was for your benefit?'

'No.' Mark shook his head slowly. 'No, I'm sure it isn't that. She looks different. Much more cheerful.'

Holly nodded. 'You're right actually. That's exactly how she looks.'

Mark grinned. 'I must ring Greg. Things are obviously going well in that direction.'

'But now that you're a hero, maybe she'll have second

104

thoughts about moving on to Greg,' Holly teased, and Mark rolled his eyes.

'Next time I jump into the water after some teenage idiot, remind me to wear a bag on my head.'

'Next time?' Holly's smile faded and she put her coffee down, untouched. '*Next time?* Please, don't tell me you're planning to repeat the experience. My nerves couldn't stand it.'

'Your nerves?' He stared at her curiously. 'Come to think of it, you were rather stressed about the whole incident. I never saw you panic when we worked in A and E. Why did it bother you so much?'

As if she could tell him that!

She didn't have much faith in her ability to hide her feelings from him, so she avoided his gaze. 'Going into cold water to rescue someone is a stupid thing to do,' she said quickly. 'Of course you scared me.'

He watched her in silence, his expression thoughtful. 'I wore a rope and I'm a strong swimmer, Holly. What was there for you to be scared about?'

Against her better judgement she glanced at him and immediately saw the speculation in his eyes. Bother!

'You're my best friend, Mark,' she muttered, standing up quickly and taking her coffee over to the sink. 'I've known you for twenty-four years.'

There was a pause. 'And that's why you were worried?' His voice was casual. 'Because you thought you'd lose a friend?'

'Of course.' Holly tipped her coffee down the sink and washed the mug. 'What other reason would there be?'

'You tell me…'

Holly's pulse rate increased. Had he guessed why she'd been so upset last night? That she'd been terrified she was going to lose him?

She glanced towards him, wondering just how much he

knew about her real feelings, but his expression was un-readable.

'You're far too handsome to drown, Mark,' she said lightly, straightening her uniform and making for the door. 'Think of all the female hearts you'd break.'

With that she closed the door firmly behind her and went to her treatment room. She was going to have to work harder at hiding her feelings or it would take Mark no time at all to work out how she really felt about him—and that would be the end of their friendship.


Monday afternoon was the family planning clinic which she was scheduled to run with Mark.

'Typical,' she muttered to herself as she got everything ready for the session. 'The more I try to avoid the man, the more we're thrown together.'

Her first patient was Anna Watts, looking a little better than she had the previous week.

'I hope you don't mind me coming.' She looked at Holly almost shyly and lifted little Harry out of his car seat.

'I'm pleased to see you, Anna,' Holly said quietly. 'How are you feeling?'

'A bit better actually.' Anna settled the baby more comfortably against her shoulder. 'My husband's got three interviews. He was so pleased about that he stayed at home all weekend so he could help me. It was bliss, to be honest. I finally had some time to myself.'

'That's good.' Holly nodded encouragingly. 'And how's the crying?'

'Your massage has worked wonders,' Anna told her with a grateful smile. 'I've been doing it every evening and he's much more settled.'

'And how about you?' Holly asked softly. 'Eating, sleeping?'

Anna looked at the floor. 'Well, I still haven't got much

of an appetite, I must admit, and I'm still not sleeping very well, but Dr Logan did say that the drug he gave me doesn't necessarily make you sleepy.'

Holly glanced at her notes and saw that Mark had prescribed an SSRI, one of the newer antidepressants. 'That's right. It isn't a sedative. But as the drug starts to work you should find that you sleep better, just because you're generally more relaxed.'

'I hope so.' Anna stood up and walked around with Harry who had started to fret slightly.

'So, what can I do for you today?' Holly asked carefully, knowing that Anna had obviously come for a reason.

Anna coloured and didn't quite meet her eyes. 'Well, I had all those problems after the birth…'

Holly nodded. 'Debra filled me in. It must have been awful for you.'

'It was.' Anna shifted Harry onto her other shoulder and rubbed his back gently. 'The thing is, I had to have surgery afterwards, and I'm wondering when I can—I mean, when it's safe to…'

'Make love again?' Holly finished for her, and Anna nodded.

'Yes.' Then she blushed furiously. 'My husband—well, now things are looking up, he really wants—he's more in the mood…'

'And what about you?' Holly sat back in her chair and watched her closely. 'What do you want, Anna?'

'I want us to get back to being a normal family as soon as possible,' Anna said simply. 'We've had so many worries for so long, I just want everything to be like it used to be.'

'But you're nervous about it?' Holly's voice was gentle and kind and Anna shifted awkwardly.

'Yes, very. The birth was so painful and afterwards…' She gave a wry smile. 'I haven't even had a postnatal check really. Actually I'm terrified of trying anything until I know it isn't going to hurt.'

'In that case, I think you should let Dr Logan take a look at you,' Holly said. 'Unless you'd rather see one of the female partners?'

Some women preferred to see female GPs for intimate examinations but Anna shook her head.

'No. I'd rather see Dr Logan. He's the only doctor I trust after what happened,' she confided, shifting Harry back to the first shoulder and jigging him slightly to calm him down. 'I don't care that he's a man—once you've had a baby and been poked and prodded down there you don't have any modesty left.'

Holly smiled. 'I'll go and see if he's free.'

She tapped on Mark's door and heard his sharp, 'Come in.'

'Mark?' She opened the door and popped her head round, checking that he didn't have a patient with him. 'Can I talk to you?'

'Of course.' He raised an eyebrow. 'What's up?'

Lounging behind his desk, he looked very sexy and more than a little remote and she felt ridiculously self-conscious. Every time she looked, she saw less of her old friend Mark and more of a very strong, virile male.

'I've got Anna Watts in my room…'

He frowned. 'And…?'

'And she wants to know whether it's OK for her and her husband to have sex.' Holly blushed as furiously as Anna had and Mark grinned wickedly.

'She wants my permission?'

'Mark!' Holly was totally flustered. 'For goodness' sake! You know what I mean.'

'Of course I do,' he said softly. 'I just like to tease you. What is it about sex that makes you so shy, Holly?'

Holly bit her lip. 'I'm not shy.'

'No, maybe not shy.' He leaned back in his chair and watched her closely, his dark eyes sharply perceptive. 'Shy's the wrong word. Just inexperienced. Under that innocent exterior I suspect you're a burning cauldron of emotions just waiting to explode.'

He didn't know the half of it, she thought, backing away towards the door, trying to remember how this awkward conversation had started.

She didn't argue with his comment about her inexperience. Her lack of serious boyfriends was no secret, especially not to Mark who'd known her for so long.

'I just need to you to examine her and see whether everything is back to normal,' she muttered, trying to remind him about the original purpose of their conversation.

'She should have had a follow-up appointment at the hospital.' Mark's mouth tightened. 'Didn't they call her back?'

Holly shook her head. 'I don't know. I didn't ask, I'm afraid. I wasn't really sure what had happened before.'

'OK.' He rose to his feet in a fluid movement and walked towards her. 'Let's go and see her. Will you chaperone?'

'Of course.' Holly followed him back to the treatment room and hovered while he questioned Anna.

'Didn't you have a follow-up appointment at the hospital?' He checked her notes with a frown and she blushed deeply.

'I was supposed to go…'

Mark's head jerked up from the notes and his eyes narrowed. 'But?'

Anna shrugged helplessly. 'I couldn't face it. I hate that hospital, Dr Logan. And I don't really trust them.'

Mark sighed and put the notes down on the desk, his expression grim.

'Well, I'm sorry you feel that way.' He gave Anna a crooked smile. 'OK, here's what we'll do. I'll give you a full examination now and then I'll write to your consultant and tell him my findings so that they can discharge you. Is that all right?'

Anna nodded gratefully. 'Thanks.'

Mark shrugged and gave her a relaxed smile. 'No problem. Holly? Can you get me a speculum and some gloves, please?'

Holly quickly set up a trolley for him and drew the curtains so that Anna could get undressed.

'Just your lower half, Anna,' she said quietly, taking Harry from her and strapping him back into his car seat so that she was free to assist Mark.

Mark washed his hands and then snapped on a pair of gloves. 'OK, Anna, just relax. I promise not to do anything without warning you. I'm just going to look at your episiotomy scar first.'

Anna tensed and stared at the ceiling and Holly gave her hand a squeeze. She always hated gynaecological examinations, too—especially by male doctors. But to give him his due, Mark was very careful and considerate.

'That's healed beautifully, Anna,' he said quietly, reaching for a speculum. 'I'm just going to examine you internally. Can you adjust the light for me, please, Sister?'

Holly reached up and did as he asked, wincing as Anna gripped her hand.

'Am I hurting you?' Mark's face was concerned as he looked at his patient. 'I need to know whether this actually hurts, or whether it's just because you're scared and tense and expecting it to hurt.'

'I—I don't know.' Anna bit her lip and held onto Holly. 'I just can't believe that it won't hurt.'

'Actually, it seems to have healed very well,' Mark said calmly as he finished his examination. 'When did you last have a smear?'

'I can't remember.'

Holly disengaged her hands and checked the notes quickly. 'Five years ago.'

'Let's do one, then. Can I have a spatula, please?' Mark held out his gloved hand and Holly passed him an Aylesbury spatula.

'That's OK, Anna. All finished.'

He straightened and stood back while Holly pulled a cover back over Anna and helped her sit up.

'It all looks fine,' Mark told her, his voice very reassuring. 'As for intercourse, well, I should give it a go and see how you get on.'

Anna went red, watching as he walked across the room and stripped off his gloves. 'You don't think it will hurt?'

Mark hesitated and then gave her a gentle smile. 'It might, Anna,' he said honestly, 'but I think it's more likely to be psychological than physical. You had a bad experience and you're naturally anxious that penetration might be uncomfortable.'

'But there's no reason for it to hurt?' Anna slipped off the couch and picked up her bag and Harry in his car seat. 'Nothing that you can see?'

'No.' Mark finished washing his hands and pulled some paper towels from the dispenser. 'But I should try a little scene-setting with your husband. Glass of wine, that sort of thing—make sure you're relaxed.'

Anna smiled. 'Maybe I'll do just that. It might do us both good. Thanks, Dr Logan.'

'How are you feeling generally?'

Mark questioned her briefly, assessing her mood, and then gave a brief nod. 'Don't forget to make an appointment to see me in another week. I need to check how you're getting on with your tablets.'

'I'll do that.' Anna left the room and Holly cleared up the rest of the equipment.

'What exactly went wrong with the birth?' She watched

as Mark dried his hands and leaned broad shoulders against the wall.

'She had a forceps delivery but the chap doing it was inexperienced and she's tiny.' Mark frowned and shook his head at the memory. 'Let's just say he was heavy-handed and he rearranged her insides. She had a sinus tract through to her rectum which was permanently infected and causing her agony.'

'And the hospital didn't notice that before they sent her home?' Holly was appalled and Mark's face was grim.

'According to Anna, they kept telling her not to make a fuss. They said that childbirth was a normal event and that she shouldn't be a wimp.'

'That's appalling! Debra said you spoke to them.'

'Oh, yes, I spoke to them.' Mark gave a humourless laugh. 'They took her back in and operated, and fortunately they did a good job. She actually shouldn't have any long-term problems. Not physical ones, anyway.'

'But psychologically…'

Mark shrugged. 'Well, I doubt whether she'll be rushing to have another child with the memory of that so fresh in her mind, and if there is a next time she'll have to have a section because they won't want her to strain that scar and risk it splitting open.'

'Poor woman.' Holly gave a shudder. 'It's enough to put you off having babies for life.'

There was a long silence and Mark stared at her, his gaze curious.

'Does it put you off?' His eyes fixed on hers. 'Are you scared of having children?'

'I— Me?' Holly stared back at him, startled. 'I don't know. I don't really think about it. Why would I? To have children you need to be in love, married.'

'And you've never met anyone that you loved enough to want to have children with?'

His voice was casual but his eyes were searching.

'My love life is non-existent,' she croaked. 'You know that.'

'And I've never been able to work out why.' Suddenly he was very still. 'Why, Holly? Why haven't you ever found anyone to fall in love with?'

Because no one had matched up to Mark. She knew that now. Since the day of the rescue, the whole of her non-existent love life made sense. It was no wonder that she'd never been able to fall in love with any of the men who'd chased her. Or that she'd never felt able to go to bed with them. It wasn't that there was anything wrong with them, or her. Not at all. It was just that she was already in love, and had been for probably all of her life. With Mark.

But she couldn't tell him that.

'Meeting the right person doesn't happen that easily, Mark,' she murmured, ripping the paper from the examination couch and lobbing it into the bin. 'You should know that.'

'Should I?' His guarded response made her glance up and she frowned briefly, confused by his response.

'Well, you've never been in love either, have you?'

There was a heavy silence and then something flickered in the depths of his eyes.

'Mark?' Holly's voice was a stunned croak and her hands dropped to her sides. 'You—you love someone?'

Her heart thudded unbearably and suddenly she felt slightly sick.

Mark looked at her warily. 'Holly…'

'Who?' Her fists clenched by her sides and she tried to keep her tone casual. 'You never said…'

He turned away from her, his tone dismissive. 'It isn't important.'

Holly swallowed hard and forced herself to ask the question, no matter how much his answer would hurt.

'Of course it's important. You're my best friend.' Her face felt strangely tight and smiling was suddenly an enormous effort. 'I can't believe you haven't told me before. Does—does she feel the same way?'

Even asking the question was painful. How much more painful would the answer be?

'No.' Mark gave a short laugh and she saw a gleam of irony in his dark eyes as he glanced at her. 'No, Holly, she doesn't. The truth is, she doesn't even notice me.'

Why was he looking at her like that? With a wry smile playing around his very sexy mouth?

'Every woman notices you, Mark.'

'Not this one.' Suddenly he sounded tired and he gave a low curse and shrugged broad shoulders. 'Forget it, Holl—it isn't your problem. I shouldn't have mentioned it.'

Holly swallowed hard again. She hated hearing him tell her how much he loved another woman. Hated it. But she was his best friend and he'd listened to her problems so often that she ought to be happy to listen to his.

She took a deep breath and managed a smile. 'Mark Logan, I've never yet met a woman who didn't fall for your fatal charm. You just need to work harder on her.' She felt a rush of concern and looked at him anxiously. 'But, Mark, if she finds out about me, she'll get the wrong idea.'

Wouldn't it ruin everything for him? Surely he didn't have a chance with this woman if she found out he had a fiancée.

'That's not a problem,' Mark murmured, avoiding direct eye contact and concentrating instead on an asthma poster displayed on her wall.

'Of course it's a problem,' Holly said, frantic to make him see that he could blow everything if he wasn't careful. 'She won't know this is a fictitious engagement, that we're just pretending, and I don't want you hurt.'

'Holly, please!' He interrupted her sharply, rubbing his

forehead as if it was aching. 'Just leave it, will you? I don't want to talk about it.'

'I'm sorry,' she said softly, crossing the room and slipping her arms round his waist. 'I just can't believe there's a woman in the world who wouldn't snap you up, given the chance. Has she guessed how you feel?'

'No.' He stiffened slightly and put her gently away from him. 'She hasn't. She's a bit naïve like that. And now let's drop the subject. I've got to finish my surgery.'

Before he could move, the door opened and Caroline entered, her tone brisk.

'Could you come quickly Dr Logan? There's an emergency.' She glanced quickly from one to the other, her expression anxious. 'It's Jack Finn. He's complaining of severe chest pain. He was waiting in Reception but I moved him into Ian's room to wait because I was worried about him.'

Jack Finn?

Mark sprinted out of the room and Holly followed him, glancing at Caroline as they hurried down the corridor.

'Have you called an ambulance?'

'Yes.' Caroline nodded briefly. 'But they reckon it will be at least half an hour because there's been a major accident on the bypass.'

'Typical.' Mark glanced at Holly. 'Grab the ECG machine and bring it through.'

By the time she entered the room with the machine, Mark was talking quietly to Mr Finn and taking a brief history.

'His pain sounds ischaemic,' Mark said quickly as she set up the machine. 'Let's give him 300 mg of aspirin, a GTN spray sublingually and then start an IV.'

Once Mr Finn had been given the aspirin and the spray, Holly handed Mark a venflon which he inserted with ease.

'OK, how are we doing here?' Mark was as cool and unflustered as ever. 'How's the pain now, Jack?'

The man groaned slightly, his skin slightly sweaty and cool. 'Pretty bad,' he confessed, and Mark's eyes flickered to Holly.

'He needs some oxygen and then let's give him some opiates and an anti-emetic.'

Holly drew up the injections and gave Mark the ampoules to check.

'Fine. Good.' He took the syringe from her with a nod of thanks and she pulled the ECG machine closer.

'Shall I start?'

'Yes, please.' Mark gave the injections and dropped the empty syringes onto the trolley. 'We need a 12-lead ECG. If it's an infarct we need to give him thrombolysis.'

Holly ran the ECG and Mark watched it over her shoulder.

'ST elevation—look.' He pointed with his pen and she nodded agreement as she looked at the trace.

'What are the rules for thrombolysis?' She asked him quietly. 'Isn't it usually given when they get to hospital?'

Mark shrugged, his mouth grim. 'Sometimes. But not if you have a strong suspicion that it's an acute myocardial infarction, and certainly not if the transfer time is going to be half an hour. "Pain to needle time", as they call it, is crucial. Check his blood pressure for me will you Holly?'

Holly inflated the cuff and listened. 'One-forty over eighty-five.'

'Fine.' Mark checked the notes and then talked quietly to Mr Finn who was lying on the trolley, his eyes closed. 'Remind me, Jack, have you ever had any stomach problems—ulcers, anything like that?'

Mr Finn shook his head. 'No, never.'

'And no bleeding disorders or any sort?'

'No.'

'OK.' Mark glanced at the ECG again and then back at

Holly. 'Let's give him anistreplase 30 IU by slow IV bolus injection.'

Holly found the drug and watched while Mark injected it carefully and monitored the ECG.

Caroline put her head round the door. 'The paramedics are here.'

'Send them through.' Mark dropped the syringe onto the trolley with the others and reached for a pad and pen. 'I just need to scribble a referral letter for the hospital to let them know what drugs we've given and that we've given thrombolytics.'

Holly helped the ambulance crew transfer Mr Finn onto the stretcher and waited while Mark finished the letter.

'Are you coming with us, Dr Logan?'

It was the same paramedic that had been at the scene of the near drowning earlier in the week, and Mark gave him a wry smile.

'We seem to be spending rather a lot of time together lately. People will talk.' He tucked the letter in an envelope and stood up. 'Yes, I'm coming with you. We need to keep him monitored with the defibrillator while he's being transferred.'

'No problem.'

Mark glanced at Holly. 'Can you ask Caroline to rearrange my patients? I'll see you later.'

Holly nodded and went to find Caroline, updating her on Jack Finn and helping her reallocate the remaining patients.

'I hope he'll be OK,' Caroline said softly. 'I really like that old chap.'

Holly smiled her agreement, thinking that whatever had happened to Caroline over the last few days it had done wonders for her mood.

She returned to her family planning clinic, but couldn't get her conversation with Mark out of her mind.

Mark was in love. She'd seen him with so many different women over the years, but he'd never *loved* any of them.

She was astonished by the feelings of jealousy that swamped her. He was her dearest friend—she should be delighted for him. But she wasn't. She was hurt and every part of her body ached with longing. A longing for something she couldn't have…

Holly was already changed for her exercise class when Mark walked in, his eyebrows lifting as he took in her appearance.

'Phew!' He gave her a lecherous grin that was pure, predatory male. 'I'm not sure you should dress like that in front of people who have had heart attacks—you might be considered a risk factor.'

She threw him a scathing look and carried on twisting her blonde hair into a ponytail. 'How's Mr Finn?'

Mark pulled a face and gave a fatalistic shrug. 'As well as can be expected for the time being. He's in the coronary care unit. Time will tell. I popped in to see our wayward teenager while I was there.'

Holly secured the ponytail and glanced at him expectantly. 'And?'

'And he seems to be doing surprisingly well,' Mark told her, dropping his bag and shrugging off his jacket. 'His lungs are clear and his body temperature is stable. They seem to think he will have escaped with no lasting damage. Except for his ego, of course. It's considered seriously uncool to jump into the sea and then half drown and need to be rescued. What time are you leaving? Have I got time to change?'

Looking at him, all she could think about was that he was in love with someone else. Someone that she didn't even know about, that he'd never ever mentioned before—who was she?

Pulling herself together, she managed a smile. 'Are you trying to wimp out of my exercise class?'

'Me?' He grinned wickedly. 'No way. You issued me with a challenge, remember? You're going to make me sweat.'

Images of what else she could do to make Mark sweat danced through her brain, but she managed a laugh, pleased that he seemed to have cheered up since their conversation earlier in the day.

Making a supreme effort, she tried to ignore the solid lump of misery that had settled in her guts.

She'd never really given any thought to the possibility that Mark would actually fall in love at some point. All the girlfriends he'd had had never bothered her, probably because Mark had always made it brutally clear that his interest in them was purely physical. But now—now there was someone that he loved...

Forcing the thought of him with another woman aside, she walked back into his room and started stuffing things into her gym bag, stopping dead as Mark followed her into the room, slowly undoing the buttons of his shirt.

'I can't believe the poor chap has had another infarct,' he said, chatting casually as he undid the last of the buttons and opened his shirt to reveal a broad, muscular chest covered in curling dark hairs. 'Talk about unlucky. And he was trying so hard to stop smoking.'

Holly's mouth dried as he let the shirt slip off his powerful shoulders and then tossed it on the bed.

'I...er...' She cleared her throat hastily. 'Yes, it is a shame. Poor man.'

And poor her, having to stand here pretending to be immune to Mark's physique. She tried not to look at the width and strength of his shoulders, or the tantalising expanse of dark hair which trailed downwards into the waistband of his trousers.

'I saw his wife while I was there,' Mark continued, his hand moving to the button of his fly. 'Fortunately they've got daughters living in the village so there's plenty of family support.'

He slid his trousers down strong, muscular thighs and stepped out of them, standing relaxed and confident in nothing but a pair of black silk boxer shorts as he continued to talk.

'It'll be a blow to the rest of the group, of course,' he said thoughtfully, frowning slightly as he hung the trousers in his wardrobe, seemingly unaware that her eyes were glued to his body.

'Yes.' She could do little more than nod, wondering what he would do if he knew what she was thinking. If he knew that she was imagining that body in close contact with hers.

Still talking to Holly, Mark reached into the cupboard for a dry towel and slung it carelessly over his shoulder before strolling into his bathroom and pulling the door to behind him.

Holly swallowed hard and sank onto his bed, trying to erase the images of a near naked Mark from her mind. If he'd guessed how she really felt he would be running a mile.

Forcing her numb brain to work, she glanced towards the bathroom, giving a low whimper as she realised that he hadn't closed the door properly and that she could see clearly through the Perspex door of the shower cubicle.

He had his back to her and he soaped himself slowly, running a hand over the smooth swell of muscle at his shoulders and down to his hip and firm thighs. Unable to drag her eyes away, Holly stared at his strong physique, her heart thudding painfully as she visually explored every inch of his fantastic body. Well, not quite every inch— thank goodness he had his back to her. But if he turned…

With a gasp of panic she scrambled off the bed and fled

to her room, her hands shaking and her breathing shallow. Thank goodness he hadn't seen her staring!

Dragging a deep breath into her starving lungs, she walked downstairs on trembling legs and sat outside on the deck, enjoying the peaceful calm of the late afternoon.

By the time Mark emerged, his hair still damp from the shower, she'd managed to salvage some of her composure and stood up quickly.

'Ready to go?'

'Of course.' If he noticed the croak in her voice he didn't comment, calmly ushering her down the stairs towards the front door.

'We'll take my car.' Mark unlocked the door for her and Holly slid into the passenger seat, careful to sit as far away from the driver's seat as possible so that she reduced the risk of physical contact with his solid thigh which rested only inches from hers. She had an all-too-vivid picture of how those legs of his looked underneath the loose tracksuit bottoms that he'd pulled on after his shower. Strong, hard with muscle and covered in dark hairs...

Oh, help!

Once inside the leisure centre she forced herself to forget about Mark and concentrated instead on making the people in her class feel confident about the exercise she had planned for them.

'I'll be showing you different levels for each movement,' she told them, adjusting her microphone carefully so that her instructions were clear. 'Just do what you feel comfortable with.'

The class was a resounding success, and as everyone was leaving Holly suddenly noticed Greg standing in the doorway, watching her.

'Were you planning to join my class?' She gave him a cheerful smile which faded as she noticed his glum expression. 'Greg? What's wrong?'

'I've had a slight crisis.' He glanced over her shoulder. 'I need to see Mark.'

'I'm here.' Mark strolled over, looking supremely fit, a sports bag slung casually over his shoulder. 'You're looking at an exhausted man. Never let me mock an exercise class again.'

'Yeah.' Greg gave a brief smile, but his eyes were worried and Holly touched his arm gently.

'Something's wrong. You mentioned a crisis.'

'Crisis?' Mark's eyes narrowed and his handsome face was suddenly serious as he dropped the sports bag on the floor. 'What crisis? What's happened?'

Greg hesitated and then took a deep breath. 'There's been a fire at my house.'

Holly gasped. 'A fire? Oh, no!'

'Anyone hurt?' Mark's sharp question was straight to the point and Greg shook his head.

'No. The builders had left for the day.' He glanced at Holly and gave a slight shrug as he explained. 'I've bought an old cottage that I'm renovating. I do some of it myself and use builders for some of it.'

Holly nodded. 'So you're not living there?'

'Well, I was.' Greg gave a rueful smile. 'I was sort of camping out in one of the bedrooms, but the smoke damage is too bad for me to stay and I was wondering…'

'Come to us,' Mark said immediately, his voice quiet and firm. 'We've got a spare room which you can have for as long as you like.'

Greg glanced from one to the other. 'I don't know. I don't want to impose but I have to admit I was hoping you'd offer. I did think of asking Caroline, but I don't think our relationship has quite reached that stage yet.' He managed a sheepish grin. 'I'd probably get my face slapped.'

'It's no imposition. We've got a spare room that's empty.

We insist,' Mark said, turning to Holly, his dark brows raised in question. 'Don't we, sweetheart?'

'Of course.' Holly licked dry lips and tried not to think about the implications. The spare room wasn't empty. She was in it. And if Mark was giving it to Greg, that would mean...

'Well, that's settled, then.' Mark wiped his forehead with the corner of a towel which was draped over his broad shoulders. 'Do you need a hand to bring some stuff over to our place?'

'Our place.' He said it so naturally. As if they really did live there as a couple.

'That would be great if you can spare the time,' Greg admitted. 'One journey should do it if there's two of us. I promise not to stay for more than a few days. I just need somewhere to use as a base while they assess the damage and I work out what to do.'

'No problem. You're welcome for as long as you need to stay.' Mark turned to Holly and took her face in his hands, giving her a smile that was for her alone and dropping a gentle kiss on her lips. 'Can you check that the spare room is ready for guests, sweetheart? We'll see you in a bit.'

Which, roughly translated, meant that she was meant to go home and remove all traces of herself from the spare bedroom. From tonight onwards she was going to be sleeping in the same room as Mark.

# CHAPTER SEVEN

HOLLY stared at her reflection in the bathroom mirror and took a deep breath. She couldn't do it. She couldn't walk into that bedroom and behave as if nothing was wrong, as if she were immune to Mark. Keeping up an act when he was fully clothed and going about his daily activities was one thing—but naked and in his bed was quite another.

She closed her eyes and shook her head. How had she ever got herself into this awful situation? She was totally out of her depth. Unless she was very, very careful he was going to guess how she felt and that would be disastrous. If Mark had the slightest suspicion that her feelings towards him had changed, their friendship would be over. She knew Mark well enough to know how wary he was of women who found him attractive. And who could blame him? He'd been pestered by members of her sex for most of his life. One of the reasons that their friendship had lasted so long was because she *hadn't* ever found him attractive. Until now.

Somehow she had to find the strength to go into that bedroom and pretend to be indifferent. She owed him that much.

Holly stared into the mirror again and tugged at her skimpy nightie, trying to make it longer. What had possessed her to buy such sexy nightwear? She sighed and fingered the cream silk fabric. She loved feminine nightwear but it was a ridiculous indulgence really. After all, who was she dressing for? Certainly not a man. She'd never felt comfortable enough with a man to let him see her in her nightwear!

Not that Mark was likely to notice what she was wearing. To him she was just the girl he'd known for most of his life. And, anyway, he was in love with someone else.

Forcing herself to accept that he'd never see her as anything other than his oldest friend, she ran shaking fingers through her blonde hair and practised a smile in the mirror. It wasn't very impressive so she tried again.

Finally she took a deep breath and opened the door, keeping the smile pinned to her face as she saw Mark lounging, handsome and relaxed, on top of the bed. At least he was still fully clothed.

'Well, Logan, you'd better not snore,' she said lightly, walking briskly across the bedroom and sitting on the bed. 'If you keep me awake, I'll thump you.'

He lifted a dark eyebrow and put down the medical journal he'd been reading. There was a long silence while his eyes travelled slowly over her, scanning every inch of her body.

'You expect me to be able to sleep? With you dressed in *that*?' His voice was filled with gentle laughter. 'That is not the sort of nightwear I imagined a virgin would wear.'

To cover her nerves she dived under the sheets and shot him a scathing look but his grin widened and he sprang to his feet and made for the bathroom.

'I'm off to take a long, cold shower.'

Still chuckling, he disappeared into the bathroom and Holly closed her eyes, relieved to have some breathing space. She really couldn't cope with his banter at the moment. She just hoped he wore pyjamas in bed.

When he finally slid into bed next to her she felt his hair roughened leg brush against hers and knew that if he was wearing anything, then it was the barest minimum.

Pretending to be asleep, she lay absolutely still and tried to breathe normally, horribly aware of his nearness. She daren't move in case she touched him and she doubted whether she'd be able to sleep a wink. Not with him lying next to her.

Holly felt safe.

So very safe and warm.

Wrapped in strong arms, she was being held firmly against a powerful chest, warm skin and dark hairs teasing the soft skin of her cheek. It felt unbelievably good. So good that she never wanted to move. Yawning, she snuggled closer, enjoying the tantalising male smell and the unusual feeling of security as she gradually woke up.

She never usually felt this nice in the mornings. And that was because—

Her eyes flew open and she was suddenly wide awake. She was in bed with Mark. She was lying on Mark. Her arms were wrapped round him.

Hardly daring to breathe, she eased away from him slowly, her heart thumping rapidly as she tried to extricate herself without waking him up. Please, please, don't let him realise…

His eyes were closed and his breathing was even but something about his stillness made her freeze and look at him closely. Was he really asleep? Deciding that he had to be—If he was awake then he would hardly be lying there, holding her—she slithered out of the bed and tiptoed across the bedroom to the bathroom, locking the door carefully behind her.

Covering her face with her hands, she gave a groan and sagged against the wall. That could have been so embarrassing! What if Mark had woken up and found her wound around him like a piece of bindweed?

Vowing to make some excuse and sleep on the floor from now on, she turned on the shower, trying to wash away the tingle in her skin that had been there ever since she'd felt his powerful legs tangled with hers. She hadn't expected to sleep a wink, but the truth was that having Mark so close had made her feel safe. Even safer than she'd felt just knowing he was sleeping at the other end of the house.

By the time she'd washed her hair and wrapped herself in a fluffy white bathrobe she'd found on the back of the door, she was more in control.

Walking out into the bedroom, she glanced towards the bed and realised it was empty but the doors to the balcony were open and she saw Mark, his back to her, staring out across the sea.

He was dressed only in a pair of boxer shorts which clung to the hard muscle of his thighs, and her eyes drifted over his powerful physique, resting on the curve of his shoulder muscles.

She frowned slightly.

He seemed tense, as if something was bothering him.

'Mark?' Instinctively she stepped towards him, concerned. 'Mark, are you all right?'

He stiffened but didn't turn, his voice gruff. 'I'm fine.'

'But—'

'I'm fine, Holly. And it's your turn to get the kettle on.'

She hesitated, wondering whether to persist, but then backed away, sensing that for some reason he didn't want her there. Which probably meant he was thinking about the woman that he was in love with…

Tying the dressing-gown more firmly round her middle, she padded downstairs, watching the sea glistening in the early morning sunlight.

Cross with herself for being so pathetic, she waited for the kettle to boil and tried to forget that finally Mark had fallen in love with someone. She'd never imagined that loving someone who didn't love you back could be so painful. But the knowledge was always there, sitting inside her like a lump of lead, weighing her down.

'Coffee ready yet?' Mark's voice made her start and she turned with a smile and a nod.

'Of course.' She reached for two mugs and made some coffee, trying not to notice how handsome he looked, dressed in a crisp white shirt, his dark hair still damp from the shower. 'Did you have a good night?'

It was small talk—just casual conversation—but the minute she'd said it, she wished she hadn't because he turned to face her and his eyes locked with hers.

She shouldn't have mentioned the night. After all, they'd spent it together…

'My night was fine,' he said softly, his probing eyes still fixed on hers. 'How was yours?'

'I slept well,' she croaked, wishing that she could look away. There was a look in his eyes that she couldn't interpret. Dear God, please, don't let him have guessed how she felt about him.

He scanned her pale face and then he muttered something under his breath and reached for her, dragging her hard against him, capturing her mouth with his.

There was no warning—no time for her to even pretend to protest.

His mouth claimed hers with a savage hunger that made her clutch him for support, sharp darts of electricity stabbing her body as his tongue skilfully explored and possessed her mouth. In one easy movement he lifted her and sat her on the work surface, his hands sliding through her hair and anchoring her head to give him better access. Without pausing for breath, he kissed her, his mouth relentless on hers, his body hard and unyielding as he pressed closer to her.

And she kissed him back, unable to resist the fire that his touch ignited inside her. Her hands slid over his shoulders, tracing the muscle of his back, and then locked around his waist, holding him against her, wanting to feel him closer, closer, hoping he'd never let her go…

But then he did—so suddenly that she moaned in protest. And then she saw Greg in the doorway.

Holly slid to the floor, her face pink with embarrassment as she straightened her dressing-gown.

She hadn't heard Greg but obviously Mark had, which was why he'd kissed her. Not because he'd found her irresistible, which was what she'd foolishly believed for one blissful, deluded moment. Disappointment sliced through her insides.

'Sorry.' Greg gave an awkward smile and raked a hand through his blond hair. 'Didn't mean to interrupt anything. Next time I'll develop a coughing fit before I enter a room.'

'No problem.' Mark's tone was short and Holly glanced at him in surprise, admiring his acting skills yet again. He sounded genuinely irritated, which was ridiculous. Wasn't he taking the act a little bit far? Surely he could be convincing without being crabby with Greg.

'Coffee, Greg?' She handed him a mug and smiled, trying to compensate for Mark's churlishness. 'I meant to ask you last night, how are you getting on with Caroline? She seems…different somehow.'

'We're getting on very well, thanks.' Greg gave her a saucy wink and took the mug with a nod of thanks before settling himself at the kitchen table. 'It's not easy but I think we're getting somewhere now. We're going for a drink at the yacht club later in the week. Caroline suggested that you two join us.'

Holly frowned slightly. Why? Was Caroline using Greg as an excuse to get together with Mark?

She glanced at Mark who seemed unusually moody and tense. What on earth was the matter with him?

'Mark? Do you want to go? When are you on call?'

Greg's eyes narrowed. 'It might not be a bad idea to go

out as a foursome. It would help remind her that you two are a couple.' He gave a wry smile. 'Not that she would have needed much reminding if she'd seen the pair of you a moment ago.'

Holly blushed again and Mark stood up, a muscle working in his strong jaw.

'Why not?' He gave a brief smile and glanced at his watch. 'I've got to make a move. I've got a medical booked in before my morning surgery. I'll see you later.'

He turned on his heel and strode through the door, leaving the pair of them staring after him.

'Ouch. I'm really sorry, Holly.' Greg gave a rueful smile and drained his coffee. 'I'll make sure I sound like a herd of elephants next time I enter a room so that it doesn't happen again.'

'It really doesn't matter, Greg,' Holly said hastily, her chair scraping on the kitchen floor as she stood up. 'I'm sorry about Mark. I can't think what's the matter with him this morning.'

'I can,' Greg said wryly. 'He's a man in love and I disturbed him.'

Holly managed a wan smile. Mark *was* a man in love. But unfortunately it wasn't with her.

On Wednesday Holly arrived at work early enough to phone the coronary care unit to ask after Jack Finn. She was delighted to hear that he was doing very well.

'Could you tell him I called?' she asked the ward sister, before putting the phone down and getting ready for her clinic.

Halfway through the morning Mark phoned through and asked her to see one of his patients. She hurried down the corridor to his room, hoping that his mood had improved.

Fortunately it had.

'This is Mrs Hunter.' He smiled warmly at the old lady

sitting in the chair by his desk and nodded towards Holly. 'This is Sister Foster. She's the best nurse I've ever worked with and she's going to work wonders with your leg.'

Holly blinked. She was?

'Mrs Hunter has a leg ulcer.' Mark leaned across his desk and tapped the keys of his computer. 'There's a report here from the vascular surgeon which you ought to read. He did a full raft of investigations, including arteriography, and concluded that she has venous disease but no significant arterial disease.'

'So she needs compression bandaging?' Holly read the notes over his shoulder and then smiled at Mrs Hunter. 'We'll bandage your leg and that should help the ulcer heal.'

'You also need to keep your leg elevated and do some simple exercise to keep your calf muscle working,' Mark said, standing up and moving round his desk so that he was next to the old lady. 'How much are you walking now?'

The old lady pulled a face. 'Not a lot. But I can potter to the end of the garden.'

Mark nodded. 'Pottering is fine. The more you can walk the better. Holly will suggest a few other exercises as well when she's sorting out your bandage. What do you want me to prescribe, Holly?'

'One of the multi-layer compression bandages?' Holly picked up the report from the vascular surgeon and scanned it quickly. 'The pharmacists usually dispense them as a pack. If you write it up I'll nip next door to the chemist and pick it up while Mrs Hunter has a cup of tea or something.'

'Thanks, Holly.' He lifted an eyebrow. 'How busy are you? Can you do that right away for her?'

Holly nodded. 'Providing the leg isn't too swollen.' She dropped to her knees and smiled at Mrs Hunter. 'Can I take a peep? If necessary I could pop round to your house and do it tomorrow instead.'

Mrs Hunter frowned. 'Can't you do it when it's swollen?'

'No. If the ankle is swollen then bandaging it can damage the skin.' Holly examined the ankle and calf and gave a brief nod. 'It's fine, Mrs Hunter. I'll just quickly measure your ankle and that will help me work out which combination of bandages to use.'

'I've been keeping it up all morning.'

'That must be why it isn't swollen, then.' She stood up and told Mark exactly what she wanted and waited while he entered the details into the computer, printed out the prescription and signed it. 'Thanks, Dr Logan. I'll go next door to the chemist.'

She helped Mrs Hunter back to the waiting room and walked over to Caroline who was sorting through a pile of results.

'Caroline, I've got to nip to the pharmacy to get a compression bandage for Mrs Hunter. Is there any chance that you could make her a cup of tea while she's waiting, please?'

Caroline put down the pile of results and smiled suddenly.

'Of course. Unless you'd rather I went to the pharmacy for you?'

Holly stared in disbelief and then quickly caught herself. Caroline certainly seemed to be a changed person.

'No.' She cleared her throat and hid her surprise. 'I'll see the pharmacist because I'm not quite sure which dressings he stocks. But if you could make her a cup of tea, that would be great.'

'No problem.' Caroline picked up the results again and then glanced at Holly. 'Oh, by the way, I gather we're meeting for a drink tonight.'

Holly swallowed. Was that why she was so cheerful? Because she was going to spend an evening with Mark?

'Yes—Greg was keen for us all to go out together,' she murmured and Caroline gave another smile. A special, private one that hinted at secrets.

'He's a nice man.'

Holly's eyes widened. Caroline thought *Greg* was a nice man! Maybe he was responsible for bringing about this change in her now that Mark was out of the picture. 'He is indeed,' she said softly, thinking that the evening at the yacht club was going to be very interesting indeed.

The pharmacist quickly dispensed the correct bandage system and Holly settled Mrs Hunter in a comfortable position.

'It's important that you keep your foot at right angles to your leg while I'm putting this on,' Holly told her, picking up the wool padding which was to be the first layer. She applied it carefully, covering the Achilles tendon and bony prominences and the tendons of the forefoot and then spiralling the wool from the ankle to below the knee.

'Oh, that does feel comfortable,' Mrs Hunter said, and Holly smiled.

'I'm just going to put an extra layer here,' she told her, winding extra wool over the tibial crest to provide added protection.

She picked up the bandage and started to apply the second layer from the base of the toes, careful to maintain fifty per cent overlap and fifty per cent stretch to ensure just the right amount of pressure on the leg.

'Goodness me, another layer?' Mrs Hunter looked surprised as Holly picked up another bandage.

'We do four layers in all,' Holly told her, using a figure of eight pattern to allow the bandage to conform to the limb shape.

'I don't really understand how I got this wretched ulcer

in the first place,' Mrs Hunter admitted quietly, and Holly glanced up at her with a gentle smile.

'Well, basically the valves in the veins of your legs aren't working very well,' she explained, 'and they allow a back-flow of blood which increases the pressure in your veins. What we're trying to do with this pressure bandage is to improve the blood flow in your veins and reduce the stagnation in the tissues. I'd like to see your leg again tomorrow, just to check that the bandage hasn't slipped, and then after the weekend to check that the ulcer isn't oozing too much and that the pressure is just right. Do you want me to call on you at home?'

'Goodness me, no!' Mrs Hunter wiggled her foot back into the oversized slipper she'd brought with her and stood up with Holly's help. 'I like the excuse to come out. My daughter always drops me and picks me up.'

'That's fine, then.' Holly pushed the dressing trolley to one side and washed her hands carefully. 'Dr Logan mentioned how important it is for you to exercise. Just some walking is fine, but if you can't manage that then just do some gentle exercises with your foot. Like this.'

She demonstrated foot extension, ankle flexion and rotation, and was satisfied that Mrs Hunter understood the importance of what she was doing.

'The other thing to remember is that you shouldn't stand for long periods if you can avoid it.'

Mrs Hunter nodded and picked up her handbag. 'Dr Logan told me the same thing. He's an excellent young man.'

Holly gave a weak smile. He was indeed.

'I'll see you tomorrow,' she murmured, showing Mrs Hunter to the door. 'Do you want me to arrange transport for you now, or is your daughter giving you a lift?'

'She's coming when she's had her hair done.' Mrs Hunter hobbled gingerly to the door and smiled at Holly.

'Thank you, my dear. I'll wait for her in Reception and I'll see you tomorrow.'

'That's right.' Holly watched her go and then turned to find Mark standing in the corridor, an odd expression on his face as he watched her. What did he want? 'Did you want to talk about Mrs Hunter's leg?'

'Mrs Hunter's leg?' For a moment he looked blank and then he shook himself. 'Oh, yes—what did you think?'

'Well, it isn't too bad.' Holly walked back into her room and Mark followed her. 'I think it should heal. We usually say three months maximum of compression bandage treatment and then if the ulcer hasn't healed, refer back to the specialist.'

'That sounds fine by me.' Mark strolled over to the window and stared across the car park. 'About tonight…'

Tonight?

'Oh, Mark!' She smiled suddenly, remembering her earlier encounter with Caroline. 'Caroline hinted to me earlier that she really is interested in Greg. We'll see how she is tonight, but it seems as if you won't be needing a fiancée for much longer.'

She saw Mark's head move slightly but he didn't turn to face her.

'No, you're probably right.' His voice sounded strange and she walked up to him, her expression puzzled.

'Are you OK?'

Was he really that worried about Caroline?

'I'm fine,' he said smoothly, 'and I'd better get back to my patients.'

Holly watched him leave the room, puzzled and more than a little depressed. Whatever was worrying Mark, she was pretty sure that Caroline was cured. Which meant that, sooner or later, Mark would realise that his life was back to normal. And she would have to make a decision. Continue to work at the practice, knowing Mark would never feel the same way about her, or start looking for another job.

Despite Mark's earlier bad mood, they had a surprisingly pleasant evening at the yacht club, and from the way Greg and Caroline behaved towards each other Holly was in no doubt that Mark's problems were over.

But hers were just starting...

How had she ever let this happen? Why had she been stupid enough to fall in love with him? She should have played the part of his fiancée and then reverted to friendship when the time came without a second thought.

At the end of the evening, her heart sank when Mark invited Caroline to join them all at his house for coffee before Greg took her home. She'd been hoping to be able to escape.

Mark was quiet and thoughtful on the short drive home and once in the house Holly busied herself in the kitchen, making coffee for everyone.

Taking the tray through to the lounge, she heard laughter upstairs and realised that they must be giving Caroline a tour so she unlocked the French doors and stepped out onto the deck for a breath of air.

'Is something wrong?'

The sound of Mark's deep voice made her stiffen. She hadn't realised that he'd left the others.

'No. Just thinking.' She stared into the darkness, avoiding his gaze, but he turned her to face him, his long fingers biting into her shoulders.

'What about? Tell me, Holl.'

His voice sounded urgent, almost desperate, and for a wild moment she was tempted to tell him the truth, but common sense intervened. He didn't want the truth. He'd be *horrified* if he found out how she really felt about him.

'You must be very pleased about Caroline,' she said, her

voice sounding falsely bright even to her ears. 'Your plan worked.'

His jaw tightened. 'It seems that way.'

Holly frowned at him, bemused. He certainly didn't look too happy about it.

'So…' She made a huge effort and managed a smile. 'I suppose we'd better start planning our ''break-up'' soon.'

For a moment he didn't respond and then with a muttered oath he reached for her and jerked her against his body, his strong arms locking her against him and his mouth capturing hers in a head-spinning kiss.

Once again his kiss swamped her senses, quenching common sense and stifling rational thought. Although it was only a matter of days since they'd last kissed, his mouth ravaged hers as if they'd been denied contact for months. And this kiss was different. Different from all the others. This time he touched her with more than just his mouth.

His hands slid to her hips and he pulled her hard against his maleness, leaving her in no doubt about the effect she had on him. His hands blatantly traced the contours of her body and before she could anticipate his movements her blouse was undone and the cool night air lapped at her bare skin.

'Mark!' She gasped against his mouth and he took instant advantage, his tongue probing deeply, mimicking a more intimate act that he had undoubtedly performed many times but which she had never experienced. Because it had never felt right. Until now. Now the mere hint of what was possible between them made her knees weaken.

Without releasing her mouth, one hand slid higher and she gave a start of shock as she felt the rough scrape of his fingers against her breast, touching her intimately for the first time.

A sharp stab of desire tore through her and she wound

her arms round his strong neck, urging him closer, urging him to take more. And still more—

'Mark? Holly?'

Greg's voice came from inside the house and with an exclamation that would have appalled his mother Mark lifted his head, quickly adjusting Holly's clothing so that she was decent.

His breathing uneven, he steadied her with strong hands, his eyes locked with hers for endless seconds before he reluctantly released her.

Barely able to stand, Holly leaned against the balcony, her face shocked as she considered the implications of what had happened. Why had he done that? Why?

That hadn't just been a kiss—that had been...

Cheeks flaming, she took some deep breaths and watched as Mark turned and strode back into the sitting room, obviously intent on distracting their guests and giving her some time to compose herself after their encounter.

She certainly needed it. Waiting for her cheeks to cool and her body to stop tingling, she stayed on the balcony, protected by the darkness. Her mind ached with confusion.

Caroline was clearly only interested in Greg now.

So why was Mark still kissing *her*?

# CHAPTER EIGHT

'IT HURTS when I go to the toilet.'

Holly blinked and tried to concentrate on what the young woman was telling her. All she could think about was Mark and that last kiss that they'd shared.

Why? Why had he done that?

She checked the girl's notes for a past history of cystitis.

Was he just making sure that Caroline was in no doubt about their relationship? Was he was just keeping up the act until they could find a convincing way of ending it all?

Forcing her mind back to the job, she tested the girl's urine, sent off a midstream specimen to the laboratory for culture and gave her general advice on managing attacks.

It was late afternoon when Tina buzzed her and said that there was an extra patient who needed to be seen.

'It's a young man—Steven Hall—on holiday, cut himself. Do you mind Holly? He's slightly the worse for wear, I'm afraid, but he seems quite affable.'

Holly stiffened. 'Slightly the worse for wear' obviously meant he'd been drinking, which could mean—

'Send him through.'

The moment she opened the door, she recognised him as one of the teenagers who had been drinking on the boat the day of Mark's rescue. His hair was dishevelled and his eyes were bright.

Her throat dried and she stood to one side to let him pass. 'You'd better sit down.'

It was either that or fall down if appearances were anything to go by.

'Thanks, Nurse.' He gave a gentle hiccup and plopped into the chair, gripping the sides to balance himself.

Holly relaxed slightly. Tina was right. He seemed affable enough. There was nothing to worry about.

'So, what have you done to yourself?' She tugged on a pair of gloves and moved closer, intending to examine his arm which was covered in a grubby towel.

'Don't touch it!' He turned from affable to aggressive in less than a second and Holly stepped backwards, her heart pounding. In an instant the memories surged into her head and panic threatened to swamp common sense.

Part of her wanted to run and hide, but another part of her recognised that one day she was going to have to face up to her fears, and maybe today was the day. True, he was drunk, but that didn't mean that anything was going to happen, she told herself firmly. He was verbally aggressive, but not physically—yet. She could handle it.

'Steven?' She took a deep breath and made her voice friendly and non-threatening. 'You wanted to see someone about your arm. I can't help you unless you let me look at it.'

He stood up and swayed slightly, obviously concentrating hard on not falling over. He smelt of alcohol and suddenly seemed to be having trouble focusing, his eyes drifting away from her as he spoke.

'I need...' He slurred his words and broke off and tried again. 'I need you to sew up my arm—that's all. I don't need you to poke it around. And you'd better not hurt me.'

Holly felt her legs start to shake, and forced herself to take a few deep breaths. Nothing was going to happen. Nothing. Mark was just the other side of the corridor. He'd never let anything happen to her. She swallowed hard. But he didn't know she needed him, did he? He wouldn't know that she had a reason to be afraid because she'd never had the courage to face up to it all and tell him what had happened.

And now she was on her own with this man. And he was very drunk. Drunker than she'd first thought.

'I need to examine it before I can tell you what treatment you need.' Her heart thudded painfully in her chest and her palms were clammy. 'How did you do it, Steven?'

She tried to keep her voice crisp and professional, hoping that he wouldn't see how scared she was.

'On a bottle, and—' he swayed towards her slightly '—I've told you what treatment I need. I need stitches.'

Trying to control her breathing, Holly backed away from him, battling with the panic that gnawed away at her insides. She couldn't do it. She just couldn't do it. She needed Mark.

'I'll ask one of the doctors to come in.'

'I don't want a doctor.' He stumbled slightly and grabbed her arm as she tried to slip past him, dragging her back in front of him. 'You'll do fine. You're really, really pretty. Better looking than any doctor. And anyway, women are more gentle.'

'Let me go!' She tugged at her arm, wrinkling her nose in disgust as the alcohol fumes hit her in the face. His fingers tightened on her and she struggled to free herself, really afraid now. In a rush of terror she was transported back to that dreadful day, to the sudden tearing pain, the awful violence— 'No!'

The door opened suddenly and Mark paused briefly, his eyes darkening in anger as he took in the scene in front of him. With a low curse he strode across the room, dragging the youth away from her in one powerful movement.

Her heart pounding, Holly wrapped her arms round her waist, her legs shaking as she watched Mark lift the young drunk, pinning him against the wall with a frightening show of strength.

Holly flinched. She'd seen Mark angry before, of course. When they were young he'd always been a bit too quick with his fists for the liking of the teachers, but she'd never seen anything like the cold fury she saw in his eyes now.

'Don't you ever, *ever* lay a finger on anyone in this practice again,' he growled, easily resisting the teenager's feeble attempt to escape.

'Let me go! I'll sue you for this.' The drunk struggled again and Mark's grip tightened.

'Go ahead.' His voice was soft and so loaded with menace that Holly wasn't surprised to see the younger man pale. 'Just don't *ever* touch my fiancée again. Or I'll give you plenty to sue me for.'

'He—he didn't really touch me,' Holly muttered, but Mark's mouth set in a grim line.

'From where I was standing it looked as though he was touching you.'

'Your fiancée—?' The young man tried to focus and then gave a drunken grin. 'I didn't know she was your fiancée.'

'Well, you know now.' Mark's tone was icy cold but Holly could see that he was back in control again. Just.

He released the boy suddenly and flexed his fingers, disgust in his eyes as he looked at the swaying figure in front of him.

'Are you sure he didn't hurt you, Holl?'

'He didn't hurt me.' Her voice was little more than a whisper and Mark gave her a quick glance, his face darkening as he scanned her pale features.

He turned back to the youth, his expression contemptuous. 'Sit down before you fall down.'

Steven sat without question, looking at Mark with some trepidation.

'So are you going to sew up my arm, or what?'

'I'll sew up your arm.' Mark walked across to Holly and pulled her towards him, slipping his car keys into her hand as he spoke to her in a calm, quiet voice. 'I want you to go and sit in my car and wait for me.'

Holly didn't argue. She didn't want to argue. She was just happy for him to take charge.

She walked quickly through Reception, ignoring the inquisitive looks she received. Once in the car park she found Mark's car, unlocked the door and sank down into the comfortable leather seats with her eyes closed.

Mark joined her less than fifteen minutes later, fine lines of tension visible around his dark eyes.

'That must have been a rush job,' Holly said, running her tongue along dry lips and forcing a smile. 'You didn't give the local anaesthetic time to work.'

'I didn't use local anaesthetic,' Mark said roughly. 'He was too drunk to notice what I was doing. Unfortunately. A bit of pain might have brought him to his senses.'

'Maybe.' Holly gave a wan smile and he turned to look at her, his dark eyes concerned.

'You're still shaking. Are you all right?'

'Yes.' Holly clenched her hands together in her lap, her knuckles white. 'It wasn't his fault, Mark. He didn't really do anything. It was me. I just panicked.'

'But he touched you, which he shouldn't have done, and that was enough to frighten you to death. And what I want to know,' Mark said softly, 'is why?'

She stared at her hands in silence, not knowing where to start.

'Look at me.' His soft command made her lift her chin and face him.

'Mark, I…'

His eyes held hers. 'Why did he frighten you so badly, Holl?'

She swallowed. 'Not here.'

Mark hesitated and then gave a brief nod. 'All right. At

home, then. But we're going there right now. It's time you told me the truth.'

'What about your surgery?' Holly glanced towards the medical centre but Mark was already starting the car, his mouth set in a grim line as he reversed out of his parking space.

'Ian's going to see my last patient and I'm not on call. Greg's seeing Caroline tonight so with any luck we might have some privacy.'

He drove her home, casting regular glances in her direction as she sat silently in the passenger seat.

Once inside the house he took her firmly by the hand and led her into the sitting room, pushing her gently onto one of his soft, comfy sofas.

'I'll get you a drink.' He took off his jacket and slung it over the back of a chair, clearly intending to go towards the kitchen, but she grabbed his hand and shook her head.

'No.' She bit her lip and patted the sofa next to her. 'I don't need a drink. Sit down. I'll be all right in a minute.'

She took a few deep breaths. She had to be all right. She couldn't carry on reacting like this every time she saw a drunk man. It was totally pathetic.

Mark sat down next to her, his strong forearms resting on his thighs as he leaned close to her. 'Is there anything you need, sweetheart?'

His gruff endearment and the concern in his eyes brought tears to her eyes. 'A hug?'

He gave a low curse and tugged her towards him, settling her in the crook of his arm. 'I want you to tell me what happened that's made you so scared. And then I'm going to go out there and kill whoever it was that did this to you.'

'I should have told you ages ago.' Holly tipped her head back against his shoulder and closed her eyes. 'I should have told you before I accepted the job at your practice. I had no right—I'm no good any more.'

'Holly, you're a superb nurse.' His arm tightened around her and his voice was husky. 'You're the best nurse I've ever worked with.'

'No.' She shook her head slowly and fought back the tears that clogged her throat. 'Not any more. It affects my work Mark, it affects everything.'

'What does?' He shook her slightly, his voice probing. 'What affects your work? Tell me what happened.'

There was a brief silence and then she took a deep breath. 'I was attacked.'

She felt him flinch and when she glanced at him his face was white and shocked.

'Holly, no!' His voice was hoarse and she felt a sudden flash of remorse.

'I'm sorry. I shouldn't have been so blunt.'

'It doesn't matter.' He let out a long breath. 'Who attacked you?'

She gave a short, humourless laugh. 'You really want the details?'

There was a long silence and when he spoke his voice sounded odd. 'Yes.' He lifted her chin his eyes were fierce on hers. 'And then I'm paying him a visit—I assume it was a him. The thought of anyone touching you—hurting you— makes me boil inside.'

She'd known he'd be angry, of course. Mark had always been very protective of her. She just hoped he wouldn't rush off seeking retribution. It was one of the reasons she hadn't told him sooner—she was a little afraid of the strength of his reaction.

'I was at work,' she began softly, surprised by how steady her voice sounded. Inside she felt anything but steady. 'It was a busy, inner-city London practice and we had our fair share of waifs and strays. I'd been there for six months when it happened.'

'You were attacked *at work*?' He sounded stunned and

his strong fingers bit into her shoulder. 'Where the hell were your colleagues?'

'They were working.' She gave a small shrug and a tired smile. 'It wasn't their fault. It was a large medical centre with twelve consulting rooms and three treatment rooms. I was at the end of a clinic when it happened. It was late afternoon—most of the doctors had gone off on calls and there was an extra patient. Exactly like today, in fact.'

'They should have had security guards if it was such a rough area.' Mark took a deep breath and his hold on her tightened even more.

'This man came in with blood pouring out of his head.' Holly's hands balled into fists as she continued with her story. 'I could see that he was drunk.'

The breath hissed through Mark's teeth. 'Go on.'

Suddenly she felt slightly sick and her hands began to shake. 'I started to clean his head and he turned on me like a madman. First he just hit me.' She broke off, her breathing more rapid. 'And then he drew the knife.'

'No!' Mark's groan of denial was the final straw and she started to sob.

'He stabbed me, Mark.' Tears poured down her cheeks and suddenly she felt herself lifted bodily onto Mark's lap, his arms locking her firmly against him as if he was trying to protect her from the memory. 'He stabbed me—again and again—and just when I thought I was going to die one of the receptionists came in for something and she pressed the alarm.'

'Oh, God.' Mark swallowed hard, his face buried in her hair, his hands holding her tightly against him. 'Oh, Holly, sweetheart.'

His anguish brought all her emotions to the surface and she sobbed into his chest while he held her tightly, soothing her with gentle words as she cried.

'Tell me he didn't get away,' Mark said softly, his voice

shaky with emotion as he stroked her hair away from her face and rummaged in his pocket for a handkerchief. In the end he gave up looking and mopped her tears with the edge of his shirt. 'Tell me they got the bastard.'

Holly sniffed and nodded, her breathing jerky. 'Two of the GPs came in then and managed to get the knife from him. They saved my life.'

'That two weeks I couldn't get hold of you—' Mark's voice was a hoarse whisper '—you were in hospital, weren't you?'

She nodded slowly. 'For some of it, yes. Then I went home to my parents. I didn't want to be on my own in the flat.'

'Why didn't someone tell me?' Mark rubbed a hand across his face and breathed out heavily. 'My mother—your mother—what the hell were they playing at? They should have told me.'

'You'd just started your new job,' Holly muttered, reaching for the edge of his shirt again. Damn. She had to stop crying. It was ridiculous! 'I asked them not to tell you. I knew you'd drop everything to be with me—'

'Damn right I would!' Mark's voice was a growl. 'And you had no right to stop me.'

'I had every right,' Holly mumbled, wiping her eyes and sniffing hard. 'Your new employers would have taken a dim view of you gallivanting off to London at the first excuse. Your mum wanted to tell you but I persuaded her to see sense.'

'I'll have words with her,' Mark muttered, raking long fingers through his dark hair and taking a steadying breath. 'I'm your best friend, Holl. I should have been there. God, when I think about it…'

'You couldn't have done anything,' Holly said logically. 'You just would have put your own career in jeopardy.'

There was a long silence and then Mark frowned. 'You said the GPs saved your life.'

'Well, they dragged him away from me and got a drip in—two drips actually.' She was matter-of-fact now, the storm of emotion suddenly burnt out by its very intensity. 'They pumped me full of fluid and did what they could to stop the bleeding. Most of the stab wounds were superficial fortunately.'

'But the others?'

Holly gave a small shrug. 'They had to remove a small section of my bowel but it hasn't caused any long-term problems. Physically I'm mended.'

'And mentally?'

'I thought I was doing all right until today.'

'You were. You are,' Mark said firmly, pushing her blonde hair away from her face, his eyes gentle as he gazed down at her. 'You're bound to feel anxious when you come up against a drunk male after what happened. How the hell did you cope?'

Holly stared down at her hands. 'I don't think I did. After it happened I couldn't sleep. Every time I closed my eyes I saw his face.'

Mark nodded, his jaw tense. 'And that's why you looked so awful when you first arrived.'

'Yes.' Holly nodded. 'But I actually did feel a lot better, being here. It was the right thing to do.'

Mark stirred and shifted his position slightly. 'Because Cornwall feels safer than London?'

'Not just that.' A flush spread over her cheeks and he frowned and tilted her chin towards him.

'What, then?'

'It was having you in the house,' she said simply. 'Having you nearby. You made me feel safe.'

He closed his eyes briefly and shook his head. 'I can't believe you didn't tell me this sooner, Holly.'

'At first I didn't want to trouble you,' she said honestly, 'and after that I didn't want to discuss it with anyone. I thought if I ignored it then it would eventually go away. I resigned from my job because I didn't dare work in an inner-city practice again and I had some time off. I did a few days' agency work but it never felt right. And then you rang.'

'Thank goodness I did,' Mark said grimly. 'And what happened to the man who attacked you? I assume the police did get him?'

'Oh, yes.' Holly's expression was bleak. 'It turned out he had a long psychiatric history and he was sectioned. I don't know the details—I didn't want to know. I was too busy battling with my own problems.'

'I can't believe you went through all this without telling me.' He put two fingers under her chin and lifted her face to his, his eyes holding hers. 'If you'd called me I would have come, you know that.'

She nodded and the tears started again. 'I know. That's why I didn't call. I knew that I wouldn't be able to talk it through without you climbing on that white charger of yours and galloping to my rescue.'

Mark muttered something under his breath and hugged her hard against his broad chest. 'That's what friends are for.'

'Yes, well, I thought I was over it until that drunk today.' Holly sighed and slid off his lap, walking over to the windows and staring out across the bay. 'What am I going to do, Mark? I can't fall to pieces every time I see someone drunk.'

'Don't be so hard on yourself.' His voice was deep and gruff. 'It's early days. The scars have barely started to heal.'

'I don't know.' She leaned her forehead against the cool

glass, her eyes burning from the tears she'd shed. 'At the moment I don't feel as though they're ever going to heal.'

She heard his footsteps on the wooden floor and then his hands curled over her shoulders and he pulled her against him, trapping her against his powerful frame. 'You won't forget, but the memories will fade and you'll start to feel safer. Maybe we ought to consider putting you through a self-defence course. It might give you confidence.'

She hesitated and then shook her head. 'I don't think I could ever fight anyone. When it happened I just froze.'

'Training would sort that out,' Mark said steadily. 'It teaches you to react, not freeze. But we'll think about that another time. Right now you look exhausted. Why don't you go and have a long soak in the bath and I'll bring you some supper?'

Too tired to argue, she dragged herself upstairs and did as he'd suggested, her head thumping from the intensity of her emotional reaction to the events of the day.

Barely able to stay awake, she clambered out of the bath and dried herself before collapsing into the bed. By the time Mark arrived with her supper she was fast asleep.

It was the dream that woke her.

The same dream that she'd had every night for the first few weeks after the attack.

Only this time the images were intensified. Everything was more colourful, more real, more terrifying.

With a moan of panic she sat upright, her breath coming in gasps as she tried to focus on the room, but almost immediately strong arms curled around her and pulled her back down into the bed.

'Shh. It was a dream.' Mark's voice was right by her ear, his deep tones soothing and very male. 'I'm right here, Holly, and no one is going to come near you again.'

Her heart still thumping, she closed her eyes and tried to

calm herself. 'C-can we put the light on?' Her voice and
body were shaking and his arms tightened.

'Does that help?'

'Yes.'

Her chest lifted and fell as she attempted to control her
breathing, and he immediately reached out an arm and
flicked on the bedside lamp. The soft, muted beam of light
spread across the bedroom, making it seem cosy and intimate.

'Better?' His voice was still rough with sleep and she
tried to fight the irrational panic that chewed away inside
her.

'Yes, go back to sleep. I'll be fine.' She ought to be able
to handle this on her own. She'd had the dream enough
times before.

'Then why are you shaking?' He cursed softly as he
stroked a warm hand over her quivering limbs. 'Dammit,
Holly, you can't believe I'd let anything hurt you? You're
in my bed and no one is coming near you—relax. It was
only a dream.'

Only a dream—maybe, but it was a terrible dream and
so real that it always left her numb with panic.

'I'm sorry.' Her trembling intensified and he swore again
and rolled her on her back, half covering her with his powerful body, this time offering physical protection from her
fears.

'God, Holly.' His voice was gruff and very male and he
swept her tangled blonde hair away from her face with
gentle fingers. 'I feel so helpless. What can I do? Tell me
what I can do.'

'Nothing.' Her fingers lifted to one warm shoulder, tracing the curve of muscle, feeling his strength. 'Rationally I
know I'm safe, it's just that fear isn't rational. The dream
is so vivid that it takes me a while to push it away.'

Mark frowned. 'Do you want a hot drink or something?'

'No.' Her fingers curled into his hard muscle. 'I don't want you to let me go.'

'I won't let you go.' His gaze was fiercely possessive and for a long moment he stared down at her.

'Mark…' Holly whispered, memories of the dream receding as she stared back into his very dark eyes. Had she ever stared into them like this before? Had she ever noticed those thick, dark lashes or the tiny creases at the corners which made him look so sexy? And the way he was looking at her made her stomach tighten and her breathing stop. He'd looked at her the same way that day at the beach. And that night on the deck.

Suddenly all she could think about was what it had felt like to be kissed by him. Incredible.

And being this close was tempting—so very tempting. All she had to do was lift her head an inch and she could touch his mouth. And she wanted to. She wanted to feel Mark's kiss again. Wanted to feel those incredible sensations that made her head spin and rational thought vanish.

Against her will her eyes shifted to his firm, well-shaped mouth, her own lips parting slightly as she imagined, as she remembered…

*He* wasn't going to kiss *her*, of course. He had no reason to—no one was watching. But what if she kissed him? Feeling slightly dizzy and reckless after the emotions of the day, her eyes lifted to his. Did she dare? Would he push her away?

'Holly?' His voice was a mixture of question and warning and, without giving herself time to change her mind, she followed her instincts.

Drawing his head down to hers, she kissed him quickly, mentally preparing herself for rejection. Nibbling at his lips provocatively, she locked her fingers around his strong neck, determined to keep him close to her. Under the tips of her fingers she felt him stiffen. Felt his shock and his indecision and instinctively knew that he was going to pull away. With a moan of protest her fingers tightened on his neck, refusing to release him, and for a moment he was totally still.

And then, with a muffled curse, his mouth moved on hers and he responded. For a few seconds his touch was gentle, matching her hesitation, but then suddenly he took control, kissing her with a hot, sexual need that sent burning tongues of fire through her whole body. Gasping, she arched against him, wanting him closer, needing to feel every inch of his powerful body. The strength of her desire stunned her and she slid a shaking hand down his warm, muscular back. Did he feel the same way? Did he?

With a smooth movement he shifted above her and she felt the undeniable evidence that he *did* feel the same way as his male body came into intimate contact with hers. She stiffened slightly as his thigh parted hers, overwhelmed by the unfamiliar sensations which drugged her ability to think clearly and respond with her head.

Then his kiss deepened and his mouth seduced hers with a fierce hunger, his touch designed to ignite a similar depth of response within her. And it did. Who wanted to think when they could *feel*? And how could anything that felt so right ever be wrong? And she knew, with an absolute certainty, that this was where she was meant to be. With this man, in his arms.

His warm hand slid down her body and cupped one full breast, teasing the dusky peak with skilful fingers, the weight of his hard body holding hers down as she arched and writhed beneath him. With a groan of satisfaction he parted her thighs, touching her intimately for the first time, his long, strong fingers exploring her with a skill that made her gasp against his mouth.

'Mark!' Her whole body ached and throbbed under his

sure touch and she twisted and sobbed in an effort to free herself of the desperately delicious feelings he arose in her.

Overwhelmed by a sexual hunger that was totally alien to her, she was quivering with anticipation, her whole body crying out for the ultimate conclusion.

Now she knew why women made fools of themselves over men, how sexual feelings could overwhelm common sense, but she knew that for her it was more than that. For her it was love. Her love for Mark came from deep within her and, despite his undeniable skill in the bedroom, it was love that drove her passion.

'Holly, Holly.' Groaning her name, he kissed her deeply, his mouth trailing slowly down her body, making her gasp and writhe as he seduced her still further with his lips and tongue.

Sobbing with need, she grasped his shoulders and drew him towards her, her body shivering under his.

He pulled away slightly, his breathing heavy and his dark eyes glittering with arousal.

'Holly.' His groan reflected an agony of indecision as he stared down at her and she felt a mix of desperation and panic. Surely he wasn't going to stop? Not now...

With a cry of protest she slid a delicate hand over his chest, feeling the steady thud of his heartbeat, feeling his muscles tense as her hands moved lower to touch him intimately for the first time.

Her heart almost stopped as she felt his strength and power, as she touched his silken heat. Part of her was shocked by her own behaviour, but the desire to know him as a man was overwhelming and she could no more stop touching him than she could stop breathing.

With a fractured groan he dropped his head onto her shoulder, his harsh moan telling her exactly how much her touch affected him. Finally he reached down and grasped her wrist, the fire in his eyes reflecting the depth of his passion.

This time there was no indecision in his gaze, only a quiet intent that made her heart beat faster, her whole body drenched with excitement. It was going to happen, she knew it was. Mark was going to make love to her.

With a hand that wasn't quite steady, Mark reached over and pulled something out of the drawer by the bed, his eyes still holding hers.

'Are you sure?' His voice was urgent and very male and she could barely breathe for wanting him.

'Yes.' She moved under him, her breathing unsteady. 'Yes, very. Please…'

With a swift movement he sheathed himself and then he lowered his head and kissed her, capturing her mouth with his as he positioned himself, obviously unable to wait even another moment. With infinite care and gentleness he entered her, giving her time to adjust to his strength and size before pushing deeper.

'Mark!' The heat and power of his possession as he surged inside her made her gasp and curl her fingers into the smooth muscle of his broad shoulders.

'My Holly.' Mark groaned her name softly and Holly drowned in the sensations that swamped her, moving instinctively to the rhythm that he set.

Suddenly breathing seemed difficult. Never in her life could she remember a time when she'd had to remind herself to breathe—until now. Never in her life had she imagined that to make love would feel like this—as if she were totally and wholly part of another human being.

In awe of the feelings that washed over her heated body, she lifted a hand and touched his face, gasping as he quickened his movements, as he lifted her hips to take him deeper.

The excitement spiralled out of control and with a soft

cry she felt the sensations explode inside her, driving her to the edge of sensory awareness. Clutching his shoulders, she cried out his name, knowing from his harsh groan that he'd reached the same peak, that he understood what she was feeling because he was feeling it, too.

Mindless, she clung to him, feeling the sheen of sweat on his powerful shoulders, aware of his harsh breathing, as uneven and ragged as her own. Then he released her from his weight and rolled over, taking her with him, his arms still wrapped around her possessively.

Risking a glance at him, she saw that his eyes were firmly closed, thick dark lashes brushing his incredible bone structure.

Mark. *Her Mark.*

Relieved that he didn't want to talk, she nestled closer to his hard body and allowed herself to relax against him, knowing that this was probably the last time she'd be able to do so. For the rest of the night she could still pretend that everything was fine.

But everything wasn't fine. Not really. After tonight how could anything ever be the same again?

Tomorrow she was going to have to face reality...

# CHAPTER NINE

HOLLY lay perfectly still, eyes tightly shut against the early morning sunshine.

She'd seduced Mark.

Dear God, she'd seduced the man.

She'd felt his indecision, his hesitation when she'd touched him, but she'd made it impossible for him to say no.

How could she have behaved like that? What had come over her?

And how was she going to be able to face him?

It was time to get up, and she knew from the way that his breathing had changed in the last few minutes that he was well and truly awake. And he was watching her. She *sensed* him watching her.

'Unless you're planning to spend the rest of your life with your eyes shut,' he murmured softly, 'you're going to have to look at me eventually.'

Holly covered her face with her hands. Overwhelmingly shy and embarrassed, she didn't know what to say. How could she even *begin* to pretend that their relationship hadn't changed after last night? It was beyond even her acting skills.

'Holly!' His deep voice rang with a mixture of exasperation and laughter. 'Look at me! If you don't open your eyes in the next ten seconds, I'll use force.'

Taking a deep breath, she lowered her hands and reluctantly opened her eyes.

'That's better.' Mark caught her chin in his strong fingers

157

and kept her face towards him. 'I want to look at you while we have this conversation.'

Holly gave a small moan and squeezed her eyes closed again. 'What conversation?'

'For goodness' sake, Holly!' He took a deep breath, hovering between bewilderment and impatience. 'After everything we did last night I wouldn't have thought you could possibly be shy with me.'

Was he joking? It was precisely *because* of everything they'd done that she was shy.

But, then, he was a great deal more experienced than she was and what they'd shared obviously didn't embarrass him in the least.

Holly forced herself to open her eyes again and her heart thudded as she saw just how near he was. He lay on his side, watching her closely, the muscles of one shoulder bunching as he supported his weight. His hard jaw was rough with dark stubble and he looked overwhelmingly masculine and very, very sexy.

'So go on.' His voice was gruff. 'Why are you so shy with me? You weren't shy last night.'

His blatant reminder of what they'd shared made her face heat and she was embarrassingly aware of every delicious ache and tingle in her body, unfamiliar sensations that his loving had induced.

'You know why,' she mumbled, her face scarlet. 'Because we—we—and I don't know what happens now.'

There was a pause while he watched her.

'Why don't you tell me what you'd like to happen,' he said carefully, the expression on his handsome face giving nothing away.

What would she like to happen?

She'd like him to tell her that he loved her, but that was ridiculous, of course. Mark would never love her. At least, *not like that.* In fact, after last night—*after what she'd done*—she wasn't even confident that he would even love her as a friend any more.

Which brought her to another problem. Mark had a sharp brain. It would take him no time at all to put two and two together and work out that for her to have seduced him—behaviour so totally out of character—she must be in love with him. She *had* to convince him that she'd just been reacting to an emotional situation. Their whole friendship depended on it.

'I want us to stay friends,' she told him firmly, mentally crossing her fingers, hoping that he'd believe her. The incredulous lift of one eyebrow confirmed that it wasn't going to be that easy.

*'Friends?'* He stared at Holly for a long time, his gaze probing. 'You want us to stay friends?'

She swallowed hard. Obviously he didn't believe that that was what she wanted at all. Which meant she had some serious work to do if she wanted to convince him. And she *did* want to convince him. No way could she have Mark knowing how she truly felt. He'd run a mile.

After all, none of this was Mark's fault. He'd tried to refuse her, but she'd seduced him. He'd just been comforting her, and she'd taken advantage, knowing that he was too much of a gentleman to refuse her. It was all her fault. If she hadn't been upset…

And now she'd put him in an impossible position, so it was up to her to rescue the situation. To try and make things easy for him.

'Of course, Mark. Friends. What else?' With a decisive movement she tried to scramble out of the bed, only to fall back onto the mattress as Mark grabbed her wrist and pulled her down again.

'No way.' He rolled himself half on top of her, using his considerable strength to stop her from escaping. 'We haven't finished talking.'

Holly squeezed her eyes tightly shut, her heart thudding as she felt his hard body against hers. This was the worst kind of torture. She really didn't need such an intimate reminder of how his body felt.

'There isn't anything to say, Mark.'

He swore under his breath. 'If you close your eyes one more time—'

She opened her eyes. 'Let's just forget it—please. As far as I'm concerned, nothing has changed between us.'

After all, that was what he wanted to hear, wasn't it? He didn't want to hear her declaring undying love.

There was a long silence while he stared down at her, a muscle working in his lean jaw. 'You're serious? You're asking me to forget it?'

She swallowed hard. 'Yes.'

His breathing was unsteady and suddenly his dark eyes were searching. Looking for the truth. 'Is that *really* what you want?'

No. But it was what *he* wanted. She knew that.

'I just want things to be how they were,' she whispered, knowing that things would never again be how they were. 'I want to put the clock back. I want us to be friends—'

'Friends. You keep using that word.' His hard jaw seemed to clench slightly. 'So what do we do about last night?'

'We forget it. Last night was my fault,' Holly said bravely. 'You never would have touched me if I hadn't been upset. You were just…comforting me, and it got out of hand.'

'Are you saying that you regret it Holly?'

Her breath was coming in rapid gasps.

'Yes,' she lied, not quite meeting his eyes. Because of last night nothing was ever going to be the same. She *ought* to regret it. But she didn't. How could she ever regret an experience like the one that they'd shared. 'We never should have done that.'

*'Done that?'* One dark eyebrow lifted sardonically. 'Done what precisely?'

Holly squirmed. Was he going to make her spell it out? 'Done…what we did,' she said lamely. 'Had…sex.'

'Had sex.' His expression was grim. 'I see.'

'We're friends and nothing more,' Holly said firmly, gaining confidence as she voiced what she thought he wanted to hear.

'Nothing more…' His tone was flat as he repeated her words, and he stared down at her for endless seconds. Then he rolled away and got to his feet in one lithe movement, grabbing his boxer shorts from the back of the chair and pulling them on. 'Well, I'm glad we've cleared that up.'

Holly clasped the sheet under her chin and stared at him anxiously. 'We're agreed, then? Does our relationship stay the same as it always has?'

'Of course,' he said grimly, yanking a T-shirt over his head with such violence that Holly expected the material to tear. 'Why should one night of—what was it? Oh, yes, sex. Why should one night of sex affect a lifelong friendship?'

'Why, indeed,' she agreed nervously, wondering why he seemed so angry. He was virtually throwing things! But…if we're both agreed, why are you so angry?'

'I'm not angry!' He swept his watch off the table and glared at her. 'Why the hell should I be angry?'

Because she'd made him do something he hadn't wanted to do? Because she'd ruined their friendship?

'I—I don't know.' She stared at him miserably. 'I just don't want things to change between us.'

There was a long silence while he struggled to control his breathing. 'Dammit, why am I doing this?' He raked a hand through his dark hair and sank onto the bedroom chair, his shoulders slumped. He suddenly looked weary. 'Holly, I haven't been honest with you, and it's time I was honest.'

Holly felt as though she'd stepped under a cold shower. He was going to tell her that he could never love her because he was in love with someone else. He was making sure that she was in no doubt about the nature of their relationship. He always did that with women, she knew he did. So that he could never be accused of misleading them. Look at the lengths he'd gone to just to convince Caroline that he wasn't interested in her.

Well, she didn't need him to be honest with *her*. She *knew* that he could never love her but that didn't mean she wanted him to spell it out. Not now. Not this morning. Not after what they'd shared last night.

'No, Mark.' She clutched the sheet to her breasts, her blonde hair tumbling over her shoulders. 'You don't need to be honest. I know how you feel.'

Mark frowned and leaned forward in the chair. 'No, Holly, you don't. I—'

'Please, Mark, no!' She clapped her hands over her ears and shook her head. 'I just can't bear to talk about this now. I just can't bear it.'

Even though she knew he didn't love her and never would, she still didn't feel able to hear him telling her how much he loved another woman.

'Holly.' His voice was hoarse and she forced herself to look at him, to mask the pain in her eyes.

'I'm sorry, Mark,' she said softly. 'I'm so sorry about everything.'

'So you keep saying,' he said wearily, his whole body tense as he stood up and strode across the bedroom, yanking open the bathroom door with a force that threatened to remove the handle. 'I get the message.'

Wincing as the door slammed behind him, Holly stared

after him, her heart sinking like a lump of lead. Was he cross because they'd made love, or because she hadn't wanted to hear about the woman he loved?

How were they ever going to salvage anything of their old relationship after this?

She skipped breakfast and drove to the medical centre early so that she could avoid seeing Mark again.

She shut herself in her room, her heart sinking as she acknowledged that the situation couldn't carry on for ever. Sooner or later she was going to have to face him.

The morning passed surprisingly quickly as she renewed dressings, took bloods, syringed ears and dealt with various minor injuries.

She was just giving advice to a tourist who'd developed diarrhoea when the phone rang. It was Mark.

'I've got a fifty-five-year-old man who's been having blackouts and chest pain,' he said briskly, coming straight to the point. 'He's got a heart rate of thirty-five beats a minute and I suspect he's got heart block. Are you in a position to do a 12-lead ECG for me?'

She swallowed. 'Of course. Send him along now.'

She quickly finished with the lady she was dealing with. 'Drink plenty of fluid, Mrs Page, and contact the surgery again if the symptoms are no better in twenty-four hours or if abdominal pain is persistent or severe.'

Mrs Page stood up, her face pale and drawn. 'Should I take any medicines?'

'Better not to,' Holly advised. 'Unless you've got to go on a long coach journey or something similar, it's actually best to let your body clear itself of the problem.'

'Well, thanks for seeing me.' The woman walked towards the door and Holly gave her a sympathetic smile.

'I'm sure you'll soon be better and able to enjoy the rest of your holiday.'

She glanced up, her body tensing as she saw Mark striding towards her, his handsome face expressionless as he met her eyes.

'This is Mr Fox,' he introduced the balding, slightly overweight man standing next to him. 'I'll be in my room when you've finished.'

'Thanks.' Holly stood to one side to let the man pass, staring after Mark with a growing feeling of despondency. Had it really been worth it? One night of total bliss seemed to have cost her the entire friendship.

'Just remove your shirt and your socks, Mr Fox.' She drew the curtain across to ensure his privacy and made a determined effort to bury her personal problems. 'I'm going to attach some wires to your chest to perform this test, but it's completely painless.'

'I hope this is a lot of fuss about nothing,' the man muttered breathlessly, shifting himself slightly on the trolley. 'Everyone blacks out occasionally, don't they?'

'It's still worth investigating, Mr Fox.' Holly smeared the electrodes with contact jelly and attached them to his wrists and ankles with the straps. 'The ECG gives us a picture of what your heart is doing. I need you to relax.'

Carefully she recorded each of the leads in turn, recording a longer tracing in lead II to act as a rhythm strip for Mark. Then she marked the tracings with a pen to make it easier to read.

'So what happened?' Carefully she attached a chest lead to the fourth intercostal space joining the right sternal border. 'What were you doing at the time?'

'Helping my daughter move house.' He watched as she attached the other chest leads. 'I was lugging furniture and boxes and then I had this crushing pain in my chest. I thought it was indigestion.'

Holly switched the machine to V setting and recorded the six tracings.

'And you've never had that sort of pain before?'

He looked uncomfortable. 'Well, I have had chest pain before, but I always assumed it was indigestion.'

Holly removed the leads and helped him sit up. 'You never went to the doctor?'

'No.' He slipped on his shirt and looked worried. 'Should I have done?'

Holly ripped the ECG tracing from the machine and gave him a warm smile. 'You're here now, Mr Fox,' she said quietly, 'That's the main thing. I'll just take this to Dr Logan so that he can look at it while you're getting dressed.'

She waited outside Mark's consulting room until his patient left and then she slipped in, her cheeks colouring slightly as her eyes scanned his broad shoulders.

Damn. Would she ever be able to see him as her friend again? After last night the answer was undoubtedly no.

'I've done Mr Fox's ECG.'

He gave a nod and reached out a hand. 'And?'

'My cardiology is a little rusty,' she admitted, passing him the trace. 'But it doesn't look healthy. 'The p-wave doesn't seem related to the rest of the complex somehow.'

Mark frowned down at the trace, following it carefully with the blunt end of his pencil. 'He's got third-degree heart block,' he muttered, shaking his head slightly in disbelief.

'What does that mean?'

'That means,' Mark replied slowly, 'that there is no electrical communication between the atria and the ventricles.'

Holly stared. 'But that would make him dead.'

'No. Not necessarily.' Mark shook his head. 'In his case ventricular activity is stimulated by an independent focus arising within the ventricles. It's an escape rhythm and it produces abnormal wide complexes on the ECG—look.'

Holly leaned forward, frowning slightly as he explained

the ECG trace. 'I can't understand why he hasn't collapsed.'

'He did collapse,' Mark reminded her grimly, 'but on
this occasion he was lucky. Now we need to treat it.
Urgently.'

He picked up the phone and dialled the hospital, talking
quickly to one of the cardiology team while she hovered.

'OK.' He replaced the phone and let out a long breath.
'I'm going to give him some atropine here and transfer him
to hospital. They're going to have an infusion of isopren-
aline ready.'

'And then what?'

Mark shrugged. 'He'll almost certainly need a permanent
pacemaker, but they'll assess that when he arrives. Do you
want to send him back to me and then arrange an ambulance?'

Holly asked Tina to arrange for an ambulance and returned to Mr Fox, taking him back to Mark, staying close
while Mark explained the seriousness of the condition.

Then she went back to her own list of patients which
had grown in her absence.

By the time she'd seen the last of them it was well into
lunchtime and she slipped quickly into the staffroom to
make herself a cup of coffee.

'What a morning.' Tina was lounging in one of the arm-
chairs, her eyes closed, and Ian was munching his way
through a packet of sandwiches. 'I'd swear that some people come on holiday just to get a second opinion from
another doctor. How can so many tourists develop ailments
the minute they arrive here?'

Ian laughed and tossed his sandwich wrapper in the bin.
'It does seem to have been unusually busy. Is it your turn
to do the lifestyle clinic tonight, Holly?'

Holly nodded and settled herself in one of the chairs.

relaxing slightly now that she realised that there was no sign of Mark.

'Has anyone heard anything of Jack Finn?' she asked, taking a sip of coffee and then wincing as she burnt her tongue.

'I popped in on him last night actually,' Ian told her. 'The cardiologists are very pleased with him.'

'That's good.' Holly took another sip of coffee and then spilt a large portion as Mark strode into the room.

'What a morning.' He looked tense and harassed, fine lines of tiredness around his dark eyes. But, then, he hadn't had any sleep last night either, Holly reminded herself, springing to her feet and fetching a cloth to mop up her coffee.

Blushing self-consciously she dabbed at the mess on the carpet, casting an apologetic look at Ian who was watching her thoughtfully.

'Sorry. Not concentrating,' she mumbled, putting the cloth back on the draining board and making for the door. 'I need to get on. See you later.'

Ian frowned. 'Holly…'

But she slipped quickly away, pretending not to have heard him, too agitated by Mark's presence to stay in the same room as him a moment longer.

Her afternoon vaccination clinic seemed to drag and the children were more fractious than usual.

'It's the heat,' Caroline murmured, dishing out sweets to a howling four-year-old who'd just been given her pre-school booster. 'It's making us all cross.'

Only Caroline didn't seem cross at all, and Holly realised that she hadn't given Greg's whereabouts a thought.

'Did you have a nice evening?' She took advantage of a break in the stream of babies to ask Caroline about her date.

'Perfect.' Caroline gave her a soft smile that left no room for doubt. 'Greg's fantastic. He came back to my place last night. I suppose we should have called you—did you wonder where he was?'

'No.' Holly managed a wan smile. 'We guessed.'

'I owe you an apology, Holly,' Caroline said quietly. 'I was less than welcoming when you arrived and you were so nice to me. I'm really sorry.'

Holly shifted uncomfortably. 'There's nothing to apologise for.'

'Yes, there is.' Caroline touched her arm gently. 'When I think about how I behaved, I'm so ashamed. My only excuse is that I was still in such a state after what happened to me that I wasn't thinking straight. I just had this stupid thing for Mark, but it wasn't real—it didn't mean anything. I know that now.'

'It really doesn't matter,' Holly said hastily, but Caroline was determined to have her say.

'I suppose you must be used to women thinking they're in love with him.'

'Yes, I am,' Holly said, her smile wry and slightly sad. 'It happens to us all at some time or another, I'm afraid.'

'But you're the lucky one,' Caroline said. 'You're the one he loves.'

If only. Holly forced a smile and changed the subject neatly. 'So what's happening with you and Greg now?'

'He's going to move in with me until his house is fixed,' Caroline told her, checking through the list to see how many more children were still due to be immunised. 'He's going to tell Mark today.'

Which meant that she could have her room back until it was time to leave, Holly thought dully. So why didn't that thought fill her with delight? After last night she should be relieved to be able to have her own space. But the truth was that she was horrified by what had happened between them—by how fast their relationship seemed to have deteriorated. Twenty-four years of close friendship seemed to have vanished in one night of passion.

It was her fault, of course. She'd seduced him. Tempted him to do something he hadn't actually wanted to do. So it was up to her to mend it.

She closed her eyes briefly and resolved to do so that evening.

The lifestyle clinic was busier than ever, and several of the patients had heard about Jack Finn and wanted reassurance. In the end Ian sat everyone down and they had a question and answer session, with everyone voicing their anxieties and the whole health care team trying to deal with the problems that arose.

Holly and Samantha sorted through the recipes some of the women had brought and Tina agreed to type them up and make them into a little book to distribute in the surgery.

After the clinic Holly made her way home and was surprised to find that Mark still wasn't home. She made a light supper and laid the table on the deck, but it was almost ten o'clock when she heard his key in the door.

Bracing herself for a painful conversation, she walked into the sitting room to meet him, noticing how his shoulders stiffened warily when he saw her. What was he afraid of? That she was going to throw herself at him again? Had she really done that to their friendship? Was this really the same man who used to be so comfortable with her?

'I wanted to talk to you,' Holly said softly, holding out a glass of wine that she'd poured earlier.

He hesitated for a long moment and then took the wine from her, his expression guarded. 'What about?'

Holly took a deep breath. 'I'm so sorry about what happened—'

'Yes.' His lips were set in a grim line. 'You made that plain enough this morning.'

She bit her lip, determined to continue. 'I didn't mean everything I said this morning.'

He went completely still. 'Which bit of what you said this morning?' His eyes were fixed on her face. 'Which bit didn't you mean?'

'The bit about not wanting to hear about the woman you love,' she said, forcing a smile and trying to look as if she was dying to hear the details. 'You said that you wanted to be honest.'

For a moment he stared at her and then he shook his head slowly as if he was trying to understand. 'You want to hear about the woman I'm in love with?'

'Yes,' she said firmly, taking a huge slug of wine to give her confidence.

He walked past her onto the deck and stared at the boats moving smoothly along the estuary.

'Why?'

His question threw her. 'Well, because I'm your best friend. I—I'm interested. And you want to talk about it.'

There was a long silence. 'No, I don't. Not any more.'

'You did this morning.'

'There were lots of things I wanted to talk about this morning,' he said quietly.

She'd never seen him like this before. Remote and untouchable. 'But, Mark—'

'Forget it, Holly.' He kept his back to her, his broad shoulders rigid with tension.

'But this morning—'

'I just want to forget this morning,' he muttered, draining his wine in one mouthful. 'Drop the subject.'

Holly stared at him, feeling as though part of her was dying inside. She just couldn't seem to reach him. He just wasn't *her* Mark any more.

'What's happened to us, Mark?' Her voice was softly

questioning, slightly desperate. 'Can we ever have the same relationship that we had before—?'

'Before we "had sex", you mean?' His short laugh made her flinch and she took a step backwards as he moved towards her. 'I don't know, Holly. Frankly, I don't think so.'

She stared at him numbly.

So that was that.

She'd spoiled everything.

Determined not to cry in front of him, she swallowed down the lump in her throat and wished that she'd never, ever forced him to make love to her. If she hadn't done that then nothing would have changed between them and they'd still be friends. As it was, by trying to have everything for just one night she'd lost everything for ever.

# CHAPTER TEN

'LETTER for you Holly.' Caroline handed her a typed envelope and Holly slipped it in her pocket with a quick smile.

'Thanks.' She could guess what it was—a response to her application for a practice nurse job several hours' drive along the coast in Dorset. She'd used the practice address instead of Mark's home because she didn't want him picking up her mail. Not that he was likely to try and stop her, she thought, walking slowly towards her treatment room.

It had been several weeks since their night together and he was still avoiding her like the plague. Whenever she entered a room, he left it; he was doing extra on-call to avoid being in the house and he'd nearly always left for work by the time she emerged from her room in the mornings.

Their friendship was in tatters and the knowledge made her ache deep inside. In the past twenty-four years she and Mark had never seriously fallen out about anything—until now.

Closing her door behind her, she pulled the letter open and read it carefully, her heart heavy as she saw that they were offering her an interview a few days later. She ought to be pleased, but all she could think of was that she'd be leaving Mark. She stared at the letter and took a deep breath. What choice did she have? Mark didn't need her as his fake fiancée and he didn't seem to need her as a friend any more either.

Without giving herself a chance to change her mind, she dialled through to Ian and asked for the following Thursday off, and then asked Caroline to reallocate her patients for that day. Neither of them asked for an explanation and she didn't offer one. She needed to sort this out for herself.

Tucking the letter back in her pocket, she called Anna Watts, who was her first patient.

'You look so much better!' Brushing aside her problems, Holly's smile was genuine as she gestured for the young woman to sit down. 'And Harry looks cheerful, too.'

'He's turned over a new leaf,' Anna told her, dropping her changing bag and all the baby paraphernalia onto the floor. 'No more screaming at night, and he sleeps all the way through. I feel like a new person frankly.'

'They do say that colic sometimes resolves itself at three months,' Holly commented, picking up a toy and playing peek-a-boo with a beaming Harry. 'He seems very happy now. A different baby.'

'I can't believe how much better I feel.'

Noticing the subtle application of make-up and the newly washed hair, Holly had no trouble believing her.

'Have you been seeing Dr Logan regularly?'

Anna nodded. 'He wants me to carry on taking the anti-depressants for now,' she said, reaching into her bag for a cloth to wipe Harry's nose, 'but after another month or so we're going to review it.'

'And how are things with your husband?'

'Great.' Anna blushed gently. 'We managed—you know—and it was fine, and he's just been offered another job so everything seems to be coming together.'

'That's really great news.' Holly was genuinely pleased. 'So what can I do for you today?'

'Well, Harry missed his second immunisation because he had a cold and I didn't want to bring him…' Anna shifted him on her lap '…so I wondered if you'd do him today?'

'Of course, although for future reference a cold doesn't usually mean that he can't have his injection.' Holly called up the notes and then went to the vaccine fridge to find the correct vaccines. 'He has exactly the same as last time, Anna. Diphtheria, tetanus, whooping cough, polio, meningitis C and Hib. And then the same again at four months.'

Anna pulled a face. 'It seems like such a lot for a small baby—I've read that some people are worried about a young baby's immune system being battered by so many vaccines at once.'

'Well, a baby's immune system is tested every time he goes out of the house,' Holly pointed out gently, 'and when he's in the house as well, when you think about it. Babies are constantly bombarded by germs. At the moment there's no medical evidence to suggest that having the vaccinations together overloads the immune system. And, of course, without the immunisations, they're at risk of catching the disease.'

Anna gave a groan and bit her lip. 'I know. It feels like such an enormous decision. I'll be glad when they're all finished. It's just one more lot, isn't it?'

'That's right,' Holly gave the injections quickly and popped the polio drops into Harry's mouth. 'Then he has his MMR between thirteen and fifteen months.'

'Oh, well, I'm not worrying about that one now,' Anna said, rolling her eyes as she patted and soothed the disgruntled baby. 'There. All over now.'

Holly asked Anna to stay in the waiting room for five minutes in case Harry had an adverse reaction to the injections and called her next patient.

'Helen!' She smiled, surprised and pleased to see the little girl she'd met on her first day at the practice. But one glance told her that the girl was feeling poorly. 'What's been happening to you?'

'She's been complaining of terrible earache and her temperature is up in the roof.' Alison Brown ushered the little girl into the room and onto the nearest chair. 'The receptionists told me that the doctors are really busy this morning so I asked to see you. I hope that's OK.'

'That's fine,' Holly assured her, picking up an auriscope. She'd been trained to examine ears so she was more than confident to perform the task herself. 'I'll just have a quick look at her and then if necessary I can interrupt one of the doctors. Does she often have ear infections?'

'Hardly ever.' Alison screwed up her face and racked her brains. 'Once, I think, when she was two.'

'OK.' Holly crouched down and gave the little girl a soft smile. 'You poor thing. Earache is awful, I know! I used to have it when I was tiny. Will you let me look in your ear, Helen? I promised to be very gentle.'

The little girl sniffed and cuddled against her mother, giving Holly perfect access to her ear. Knowing that she wouldn't be given the opportunity for a leisurely examination, she worked as quickly as possible, wincing slightly as she saw the bulging eardrum. No wonder the child was in pain.

'It's very red, Mrs Brown,' she murmured, popping the auriscope back onto the tray. 'That's definitely the problem.'

'Oh, dear.' Alison looked guilty. 'She's had it for a few days but I was hoping it would clear up by itself. Should I have brought her down sooner?'

'No, not really.' Holly entered the results of her examination into the computer and then paused to give Alison her full attention. 'Most cases of otitis media—that's the medical name for an ear infection—are mild and will resolve on their own with just some pain relief. Unfortunately a small number don't resolve on their own, and those cases need to be given antibiotics. What normally happens in this practice is that in a child of Helen's age, with her symptoms, they advise you to use Calpol for the first two days to see if it resolves by itself.'

Alison pulled a face. 'She's been complaining for a couple of days already.'

Holly nodded. 'So what we need to do is give her a short course of antibiotics. I'll just see if one of the doctors is free.'

After asking Tina, she was hugely relieved that it was Ian who strode into the room a few minutes later and not Mark.

'What can I do for you?' He smiled at her with his usual warmth and listened as she quickly outlined the problem. 'So you think she needs some antibiotics?'

'She's had earache for two days already,' Holly told him, trying not to dwell on how much she'd hate to leave the practice. 'Her ear drum is red and bulging. I thought maybe she should have a course of amoxicillin?'

He nodded briefly. 'I'll take a quick look myself, although I'm sure you're right. Hello, trouble.' He crouched down and touched Helen's face gently. 'What have you been up to, then?'

Gently and skilfully he checked the ear and then nodded. 'Yes, I agree.' He straightened and slipped the auriscope into his pocket. 'Have you run off a prescription for me?'

Holly nodded and handed it to him to sign.

'Keep up the Calpol,' Ian advised, handing Alison the prescription, 'and you can try wrapping a warm hot-water bottle in a towel and holding it next to her ear. She might find that soothing. If she's no better in two days, bring her back.'

Alison nodded gratefully. 'Thanks so much, Dr Hughes.'

Holly showed them out, aware that Ian seemed in no hurry to leave the room.

Closing the door carefully, she turned back to face him and looked at him warily, wondering what he wanted.

'You look pale,' he said gruffly, his heavy, dark brows

locked in a frown. 'Are you going to tell me what's going on?'

Holly blushed. 'I don't know what you mean.'

Ian hesitated and thrust his hands in his pockets, his eyes gentle. 'Holly, why do you need the day off on Thursday?'

Holly hesitated. How could she not tell him the truth? He was the senior partner. 'I'm sorry to do this to you but I'm going for an interview.'

'I see.' Ian rubbed his chin. 'And does Mark know?'

Holly shook her head. 'No. Not yet.'

'Have the two of you got problems? I didn't want to interfere, but I've noticed things have been strained between you for a while now.'

Holly took a deep breath and nodded, not trusting herself to speak in case she burst into tears.

Ian sighed. 'Do you still love him?'

'With all my heart,' Holly said simply, her voice choked and her eyes brimming despite her efforts to control her emotions.

'And when did you last tell him that?' Ian's voice was soft and she stared at him, blinking back the tears.

The answer was never, of course, but, then, Ian didn't know the whole story.

'Holly, I don't know what's happened between the two of you,' Ian said quietly, 'but one thing I do know, by virtue of my age, is that nothing is ever gained by running away. Whatever is wrong, tell Mark how you feel. Tell him exactly how you feel. That way there can be no misunderstandings between you. If things can't be mended then so be it, but at least you will both be clear about how each of you feels.'

Holly stared at him. Tell Mark how she felt?

To tell Mark how she felt would mean admitting that she loved him—something that she'd been hiding from him from the first day he'd kissed her.

But why shouldn't she tell him? She'd been protecting their friendship, but their friendship was history now, so maybe honesty on her part would at least clear the air between them.

What did she have to lose?

Holly knew something was wrong the moment Mark walked into the house that evening.

For a start he was early, and since the night they'd spent together Mark had never been home before she was in bed. And if that hadn't been enough of a clue, the look on his face when he walked through the door would have been.

'What the hell is going on?' He strode onto the deck, his dark eyes so stormy that Holly took a step backwards.

'What do you mean?'

'Oh, come on, Holly!' He lifted his hands in an impatient gesture. 'Ian tells me you're leaving. You've got an interview at another practice!'

'Oh.' Holly's chin lifted and she frowned slightly. 'Ian had no right to tell you that.'

'Holly, you're supposed to be my fiancée,' Mark reminded her grimly. 'He had every right.'

'Well, I thought the time had come to end the pretence,' Holly said quietly, and he gave a humourless laugh.

'Ironic, isn't it?' He paced across the deck, his broad shoulders tense. 'We were so convincing that they're all but sending us to marriage guidance. Ian's reading me the Riot Act, asking how I can let a girl like you slip through my fingers. So why are you doing it? Why are you taking another job?'

Holly swallowed and gave him what she hoped was a casual smile. 'I thought I was making it easier for you. You don't need a fiancée any more.' She shrugged slightly and tucked a strand of hair behind her ear in a nervous gesture.

'As you said, we were convincing. But we achieved what we set out to achieve. It's over now.'

There was a long silence and he stopped pacing, a muscle working in his dark jaw.

'We still need a practice nurse.' His tone was flat and she turned to stare out across the bay, catching her hair in her palm as the wind tossed it against her face.

'But you don't need me. Practice nurses are two a penny, Mark.' She pinned her gaze on a small passenger ferry rather than look at him. 'You'll find someone else.'

'I don't want to find anyone else.' Suddenly he sounded incredibly tired and she wondered why having to find a new practice nurse should bother him so much. It didn't make sense.

'I can't stay,' she said finally, moistening dry lips with the tip of her tongue. His recruitment problems weren't her concern. 'It's out of the question. You must know that.'

There was a long silence and with a low curse he closed the distance between them, putting his hands on her arms and turning her to face him. 'Because of the night we spent together?'

She swallowed and looked away, blinking back tears. So, did she tell him the truth or not? Did she take this opportunity to open her heart to him for the last time, or did she hold back her feelings?

'No,' she said finally, 'not just because of that.'

His fingers tightened on her arms. 'Why, then?'

'Because things have totally changed between us and I can't bear it!' She lifted her hands helplessly and gritted her teeth. She wasn't going to cry. She wasn't. 'We've been friends for so many years, Mark, and suddenly you can't even bear to be in the same room as me.'

His hands dropped to his sides and his eyes were wary. 'That's not true—'

'It *is* true!' She turned on her heel and walked away from

him, wrapping her arms round her body in a protective gesture. 'I walk into a room, you leave it. You stay late in the surgery. You sail whenever you have a spare five minutes. We never go out together. You name it, we don't do it any more. I can't carry on like this.'

There was a long silence and she could sense his gaze on her as she waited for his reaction.

'So what happens to our friendship?' His voice was hoarse and she turned to face him, her green eyes full of sadness.

'I don't know. I thought that what we had would last for ever. I thought that nothing could *ever* damage our friendship.' She forced the words past the enormous lump in her throat. 'But I was wrong.'

He exhaled sharply. 'Holly—'

'Answer me one question Mark.' She lifted her chin bravely and stared him straight in the eye. 'Why did one night of sex kill a lifetime of friendship? I've asked myself the question over and over again and I can't come up with a reasonable answer.'

His flinched visibly and when he spoke his voice was rough. 'Sex always changes things, Holly.'

'No.' She shook her head vigorously. 'I *know* that's not true. You've slept with plenty of women and stayed friends with them.'

The skin darkened over his angular cheekbones. 'Holly, for goodness' sake…'

'Well, it's true,' she said awkwardly, blushing furiously. 'And you've definitely been to bed with women you haven't been in love with because you've told me so.'

'I obviously talk too much,' Mark muttered, raking long fingers through his dark hair and looking decidedly uncomfortable. 'Is there a point to this character assassination?'

'It isn't a character assassination.' She swallowed hard, thoroughly embarrassed. 'I just thought that men were supposed to be different from women. I thought that men could have sex without emotional involvement. I thought they could separate the physical from the emotional.'

Mark took a deep breath. 'Well, I suppose that's true sometimes, but I don't see—'

'So why did one night of sex ruin our friendship?' Holly took a deep breath and faced him bravely. 'Why weren't you able to just treat it as a one off physical experience? Was it because *I* was the one who seduced *you*? Were you angry because you didn't really want to—'

His hand dropped to his side and he stared at her in stunned amazement. 'You seduced me?' He looked dazed and shook his head slightly. 'You think *you* seduced *me*?'

She bit her lip, her cheeks scarlet as she remembered her own behaviour. How she'd touched him, reached for him, tempted him when he'd hesitated… 'Of course I seduced you. I was the one who kissed you.'

'Only after I'd kissed you a hundred times first,' Mark muttered, his breathing slightly uneven.

'That was different,' she said quietly. 'You were kissing me because we had an audience.'

'Like hell I was.' There was a long pause and he took a deep breath, closing his eyes briefly. When he opened them his expression was calm and resigned. 'I didn't kiss you because we had an audience, Holly. I kissed you because I was dying to kiss you. I kissed you because I couldn't stop myself.'

She stared at him, her eyes wide, her heart suddenly pounding wildly in her chest.

What was he saying?

'I don't understand…'

'No, I know you don't, but it's time you did. It's time I told you the truth.' Mark gave a long sigh and walked across the deck, the breeze touching his dark hair. 'Do you remember the conversation we had when I told you that I was in love with someone?'

Remember? She'd thought of very little else since.

'Of course.' She waited expectantly but he seemed to be struggling to find the right words. 'And I'm waiting for you to tell me about it. You're the one who's always saying that we don't have secrets.'

'Oh, I but I do have a secret, Holly.' He gave a wry smile that was loaded with self-mockery. 'I have a massive secret. But you haven't wanted to share it with me.'

Holly felt a flash of guilt. It was true. She hadn't wanted to hear about the woman he loved.

She lifted her chin and met his eyes bravely. 'I've already said that I'm sorry about that. I want to share it now. I want you to tell me about the woman you're in love with.'

There was a long silence as he stared down at her, a muscle flickering in his hard jaw.

'Do you? Well, maybe I should do just that. As you're leaving and our friendship appears to be in tatters, I've got nothing to lose, have I?'

'Nothing.' She nodded agreement and swallowed hard. 'So, go on, then. From the beginning.'

'From the beginning?' Mark took a deep breath and moved away from her, leaning on the balcony and staring out across the estuary, his expression unreadable. 'The beginning was a long time ago.'

She felt a twist of jealousy that he'd been in love with someone for a long time and she'd never even guessed. 'How long?'

There was a long pause. 'I first met her when I was four and she was two.'

Holly froze and the blood thundered in her ears. What was he saying?

'We played together constantly. She was like my shadow.' Mark kept his gaze on the estuary, only his vice-like grip on the balcony betraying how tense he was. 'And it didn't matter what I did, she still loved me. I put sand down her nappy, a snake round her neck, and I even cut off her pigtail to try out my new Swiss army knife. But none of that seemed to make a difference. As we grew up we just became closer. I didn't realise that I loved her then, but I knew that what we had was special.'

Her mouth dried and her voice was little more than a croak. 'Mark?'

'We had the best friendship that two people could possibly have,' he said softly, finally turning to face her. 'Over the years I had numerous other relationships—tried really hard to find that special someone—but I never succeeded and I couldn't work out why. Until the first time I kissed her. And then I realised that the reason I'd never found the right woman was because I was looking in the wrong place. The right woman had been under my nose for most of my life—I just hadn't noticed her before.'

Her breathing was ragged. 'I thought you kissed me because Caroline was watching—because you were trying to prove to her that we were together.'

'I did,' he muttered softly, the expression in his dark eyes revealing his feelings even more clearly than his words had. 'That was exactly why I kissed you the first time. But I kissed you twice that evening, Holly, and the second time was because I couldn't stop myself. Not because we had an audience. And the time after that. And after that…'

She felt hot and cold together and her knees started to tremble. 'Mark…'

'And I blew it.' He walked across to her and cupped her face in his hands, his face showing signs of tiredness and strain as he stared down at her. '*I* ruined our friendship Holly, not you. The moment I kissed you, I wanted more. Suddenly our friendship wasn't enough—I wanted you as my lover. As my partner in life. But that wasn't what you wanted. You wanted to maintain what we had at all costs and I tried to respect that, but I failed dismally.'

Her heart started to thump erratically. 'I was so sure you only kissed me because of Caroline.'

'As I said, just the once. Just that first time.' He shook his head with a wry smile. 'I saw Greg remove her some time during that first kiss. But I found I didn't want to stop kissing you.' He lifted a hand and cupped her cheek gently. 'I realised that I was in love with you and probably had been for ever. If you'd been anyone else I would have just dived right in and had my wicked way with you straight away, but I couldn't do that because it was you.'

She couldn't believe she was hearing this. 'Wh-what was different about me?'

'Our friendship.' He gave a wry smile. 'I was playing for high stakes. You were my best friend. If I'd told you how I felt and you didn't feel the same way, I might have ruined the best friendship I'd ever had. You kept telling me that you were immune, remember?'

She still couldn't allow herself to believe what she was hearing. 'You—you *wanted* to kiss me? Really?'

'Holly,' he murmured softly, 'I was *desperate* to kiss you.'

'Oh.' She blushed frantically and bit her lip. 'But you never seemed very affected when we kissed. You didn't look affected.'

He gave a wry smile. 'Maybe you weren't looking in the right place—believe me, I felt a lot.'

There was a long silence and she stared at him, her heart pounding away in her chest. 'That night we—' She broke off, blushing slightly. 'You didn't really want to—I mean, you hesitated.'

'Because I wasn't sure how you really felt about me,' he confessed softly. 'You turned to me for comfort and that's what I should have given you, but we got carried away.

was so upset about what happened to you—about what you'd been through. I tried to be just a friend to you that night but I wanted you so much, and suddenly you seemed to want me.'

'So if you wanted to…make love—' she stumbled over the words 'Why were you so cross afterwards?'

'Several reasons.' His eyes held hers. 'I was angry with myself for not having more control. I was angry with you for not collapsing in my arms and declaring undying love. I was hurt that you still wanted to be friends when I wanted so much more than that. And I was angry because you described it as sex. As if what had happened between us could have happened between anyone. It wasn't just sex, Holly,' he said softly. 'Not for me. That night I made love for the first time in my life.'

'Oh, Mark!' Her eyes filled and she shook her head, unable to believe what she was hearing.

'And to make matters worse, you made it clear that you wished it had never happened.' Mark brushed away a stray tear from her cheek with a gentle finger.

'I was trying to make things easier for you,' she whispered. 'I thought that you were regretting it.'

'The only thing I regretted was making love to you when you were emotionally vulnerable,' he murmured, his mouth tilting into a wry smile. 'I took advantage and I felt hideously guilty afterwards.'

Suddenly Holly felt an incredible lightness in her chest. 'So the woman that you told me you were in love with…' She gazed at him steadily. 'You're saying it's me?'

'Haven't I made myself clear? I'd better spell it out.' His strong fingers bit into her shoulders. 'Holly Foster, I love you. I love you with all my heart. Not as a friend loves a friend, but as a man loves a woman. I know that isn't what you want, but that's the way it is.'

'It *is* what I want,' she said softly, reaching up and touching his face with shaking fingers. 'I want you to love me the way that a man loves a woman.'

He went completely still and his eyes blazed into hers. 'But you wanted our friendship to stay the same. You were adamant about that.'

'Because that's what I thought you wanted,' she confessed. 'You hate it when women drool over you. I thought if you knew how I felt then our friendship would have been over.'

'And how *do* you feel?' His voice was hoarse and his fingers tightened. 'You still haven't told me.'

Her smile was soft and womanly. 'Mark, it was the same for me. The moment you kissed me that night in the cave I knew I loved you. The truth is I've probably loved you for ever.' Her fingers slid over his broad shoulders and curled into the front of his shirt. 'You were the reason I never had a proper boyfriend. Until that night with you, I'd never felt comfortable enough with a man to—to…'

'Don't! I don't even want to think about you with any other man,' he groaned, sinking his hands into her hair and tilting her face to his. 'That night was amazing. *You* were amazing—'

'So were you.' She melted against him as his mouth came down on hers and he kissed her thoroughly.

'And I can't wait to do it again.' He lifted his head and gave her a wicked smile. 'I love you.'

'And I love you, too,' she whispered. 'I thought you'd guessed how I felt about you.'

'I wondered occasionally,' he admitted, touching her cheek with his fingers, 'but I was so desperate for you to fall in love with me that I decided it was just wishful thinking. That and the fact that you'd never really had a sexual relationship with a man before.'

Holly coloured. 'I couldn't believe the way you made me feel.'

'I know.' He gave her a slow wink that made her heart tumble in her chest. 'It was scary, and I was afraid that what you were feeling was just physical.'

'It wasn't.' Her eyes held his. 'I was desperate for you to make love to me—but that was because I was totally and utterly in love with you.'

He bent his head and kissed her gently. 'I must be the luckiest man on earth because I'm marrying a woman I've already been in love with for twenty-four years.'

Her heart stopped and she gave a little gasp. 'You're asking me to marry you?'

'No.' He grinned at her, totally relaxed now, all the tension gone from his powerful frame. Suddenly he seemed boyish and like the old Mark. 'Not until we're standing on a sandy beach. That was your fantasy, remember?'

Holly could barely contain the happiness that bubbled inside her. 'I'm hardly likely to forget. Mark...' She swallowed hard. 'Do really want to marry me? You were always so wary of marriage.'

'Because I was saving myself for the right person,' he said softly, 'and that person is you. So what do you say, Holly? Will you love me, comfort me, honour me and keep me, in sickness and in health until death us do part?'

She stood on tiptoe and kissed him gently, her eyes filled with love. 'Always and for ever, Mark. Always and for ever.'

**Modern Romance**™
...seduction and
passion guaranteed

**Tender Romance**™
...love affairs that
last a lifetime

**Sensual Romance**™
...sassy, sexy and
seductive

**Sizzling Romance**™
...sultry days and
steamy nights

**Medical Romance**™
...medical drama on
the pulse

**Historical Romance**™
...rich, vivid and
passionate

*29 new titles every month.*

*With all kinds of Romance for
every kind of mood...*

MILLS & BOON®

*Makes any time special*™

MAT3

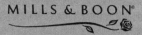

# Coming Home

*Scandal drove David away*
*Now love will draw him home . . .*

# PENNY JORDAN

## Published 21st September

# FREE
# 4 BOOKS
## AND A SURPRISE GIFT!

We would like to take this opportunity to thank you for reading this Mills & Boon® book by offering you the chance to take FOUR more specially selected titles from the Medical Romance™ series absolutely FREE! We're also making this offer to introduce you to the benefits of the Reader Service™ —

* ★ FREE home delivery
* ★ FREE monthly Newsletter
* ★ FREE gifts and competitions
* ★ Exclusive Reader Service discounts
* ★ Books available before they're in the shops

Accepting these FREE books and gift places you under no obligation to buy; you may cancel at any time, even after receiving your free shipment. Simply complete your details below and return the entire page to the address below. ***You don't even need a stamp!***

**YES!** Please send me 4 free Medical Romance books and a surprise gift. I understand that unless you hear from me, I will receive 6 superb new titles every month for just £2.49 each, postage and packing free. I am under no obligation to purchase any books and may cancel my subscription at any time. The free books and gift will be mine to keep in any case.

MIZEC

Ms/Mrs/Miss/Mr ..................................................Initials ...................................................

BLOCK CAPITALS PLEASE

Surname ...................................................................................................................................

Address ....................................................................................................................................

...................................................................................................................................................

.......................................................Postcode ...................................................

**Send this whole page to:**
**UK: FREEPOST CN81, Croydon, CR9 3WZ**
**EIRE: PO Box 4546, Kilcock, County Kildare (stamp required)**